Swimmer Boy

Third Edition, 2018

ISBN: 9781980765110

Jay Argent
jay@jayargent.com

www.jayargent.com

Swimmer Boy

Jay Argent

Prologue

Lying in his cozy bed, Liam Green opened his eyes.
Yawning, he stood and looked out the window. As a
large red truck turned onto Maple Street, a group of
teenagers walked along the road, carrying their sports
bags as they headed downtown. Liam picked up a t-
shirt from a pile of clothes on the floor and pulled it on
absently while he gazed at the teenagers, especially the
blond one in the middle. They were laughing and
looked happy. These were the last days of summer, and
the sun was shining in the clear, blue sky.

Liam winced as the brakes of the truck produced a
loud hiss. Two older men jumped out of it and opened
the back doors. Sincere joy came onto Liam's face when
he saw his beloved friend: his Yamaha Celviano electric
piano.

Finally they brought it, he thought and began to hurry, looking for his sheet music in the plastic containers stacked in his small bedroom.

Soon, Liam sat at his newly arrived piano and sang Bert Kaempfert's "Strangers in the Night" in his angelic voice. His petite fingers glided lightly across the keyboard of the piano. "Something in your eyes was so inviting. Something in your smile was so exciting. Something in my heart told me I must have you."

In the next room, Liam's parents were folding their clothes and placing them into a big, dark wardrobe. Listening to their son, they looked at each other and smiled. Moving to Fairmont was turning into one of the best decisions they had ever made.

Chapter 1

It had rained, and the air felt fresh when Liam left his home on Monday morning. The autumn sun was shining, warming the excited boy. It was his first day at his new high school, and since the school was nearby, he decided to walk; he didn't have a car, so his options were limited. Liam enjoyed the voices and the sounds of this relatively small town in the countryside. On his way, he saw many houses with happy families inside, nicely decorated gardens full of beautiful flowers, and easygoing people driving to work.

I hope someday I will live in such a house, Liam dreamed as he saw the white roses growing in the front yard of his new neighbor.

Soon, the massive main building of Fairmont High School was in front of him. Two boys were walking to the red brick building from the parking lot. One of them, tall and slim with blond hair, glanced at Liam as they passed.

I'm gonna love this school. Liam couldn't help smiling as he looked at the blond boy's handsome face and athletic body. He followed the boys from a safe distance and continued to gaze at the blond one. Unfortunately, their paths diverged when Liam entered the administration building.

Liam hadn't even told his best friend, Matthew, that he was gay. He didn't believe Matthew, or anyone else, suspected it. Still, after Matthew's family had moved, Liam's last year at his old school had been lonely.

The whole thing with Matthew was one big mystery. They had been close friends for the entirety of their young lives, and soon after their freshman year, Matthew vanished and had never spoken to him again. No phone call, no email, nothing.

Liam didn't understand why Matthew had cut him off so completely. Nothing had happened between them that would have explained the sudden change in their friendship, and Liam was sure Matthew wasn't aware of how attracted Liam had been to him.

I hope everything is okay with him, Liam thought, and a concerned expression grew on his face.

Liam opened the door to the principal's office. The secretary asked him to sit down and wait while she informed the principal of his arrival. The room was old-fashioned and oddly scary. The furniture was decades old and made of dark wood, and the pungent smell of stale cigarettes filled the space. One of the walls was full of paintings portraying elderly males whom Liam assumed to be the former principals of Fairmont High.

Suddenly, the figure in the rightmost painting opened the office door. "I am Principal Summers," the man said. "Mr. Green, would you follow me into my office, please?"

Liam stifled a grin before the principal could see it. The man was as formal as he had expected.

"Mr. Green," Principal Summers began, looking at Liam before he continued, "welcome to Fairmont High School." His greeting wasn't enthusiastic or welcoming, but formal and clinical.

"Thank you, sir. It's nice to be here," Liam replied.

Principal Summers raised his head from his papers, looking surprised like he hadn't expected an answer. He nodded quickly before focusing his attention back on the documents.

The meeting was over in five minutes, and Liam found himself in classroom A221, on the second floor of the main building. The timetable the principal had given him indicated that his first class in his new high school was about to start.

His old school had been much smaller than this one. Liam remembered the many times he had played board games with Matthew in the cozy library in the school's basement where the old librarian had always smiled at them—maybe because they were the only boys who ever visited the library. Even more than board games in the library, Liam had enjoyed playing Twister with Matthew when Matthew's sister was kind enough to let them use the game. It had started as innocent play, but pretty soon, Liam began to enjoy the physical closeness with Matthew.

Pushing the thoughts about Matthew aside, Liam picked a random desk in the second row. Sitting in the first row would have made him look a nerd and he didn't feel like one. He had to admit that he excelled in most classes and wasn't too interested in sports. That didn't sound like a nerd at all, did it? On the other hand, Liam did wash his hair daily and wore nice clothes. Maybe his gayness concealed some of his geekiness.

As Liam was trying not to overanalyze his behavior and looks, the blond jock he had seen in the yard entered the room. Liam stopped breathing and carefully followed the boy of his dreams with his gaze. The jock had a confident but friendly smile on his face. Sadly, he wasn't smiling at Liam. The jock scanned the classroom, looking for an empty desk. Liam's heart stopped when he saw an empty desk next to Liam's and started to walk toward it. But it was too good to be true; a shorter boy and a girl in a pink sweater, both of whom had entered the class with the blond boy, led him to the back row. Liam's sad heart started to beat again as he exhaled heavily.

The class was rather uneventful. The history teacher, Mr. Timothy, gave an introduction to the course, and the only interruption to his monolog happened when the classroom door suddenly opened and a red-haired boy walked casually in.

"Well, well, Mr. Taylor has finally arrived," the teacher said with a fair amount of irritation in his voice.

"Yeah, sorry. My alarm clock wasn't working," the boy said as he walked toward the last row, where his friends were waiting for him.

"Sam, make sure this is the last time," Mr. Timothy replied, trying in vain to take some control over the situation.

"Whatever," Liam heard Sam say. Evidently, Sam Taylor was a troublemaker. To his horror, Liam noticed Sam sat next to the blond jock and they said hello to each other.

Later the same day, Alex Wesley was standing in front of the Fairmont High School Swimming Hall with his friend, Rick. It was a brand new building located half a mile from the campus, next to the baseball stadium. They were playing with a shabby baseball they had found a moment earlier, and there seemed to be some excitement in the air that wasn't coming from the ball game.

"I wish he'd get here already," Rick said as he kicked the ball anxiously. He cursed when it hit the door of an old car parked in the shadow of a big basswood. Luckily, nobody saw or cared.

"Don't worry. I'm sure Sam can manage it," Alex reassured his best friend.

Their teammate had stopped at the store to get beer for their end-of-summer party. Sam wasn't old enough to buy it, but it was hardly difficult to convince Maggie Pearson to buy him some. The old granny had nothing better to do than spend her leisure time at the mall, and to the elderly woman, the red-haired, bad-tempered jock could be quite intimidating.

I wish Sam doesn't make her pay for the beers, Alex thought, and his smile faded away.

When Alex was younger, he had often helped Maggie carry her groceries to her beautiful mansion near Freeborn Lake. The Pearsons were clearly wealthy, and no matter how hard Alex tried to resist taking money for such a simple task, he had always been generously rewarded for his help. Some years later, Mr. Pearson died, and Maggie was left alone.

"I hope he brings enough drinks," Rick said.

"C'mon. It's Sam," Alex said and laughed. Sam had never failed when it came to buying enough alcohol.

Fairmont High was well-known for its baseball team, the Fairmont Predators, but the swim team was pretty okay, too. There were plenty of talented athletes, but the swimmers were most famous for their parties. As juniors, this would be the second end-of-summer party for Alex and Rick.

The boys heard the sound of a car and turned toward the parking lot. Coach Hanson parked his black BMW and began walking toward them. He was in his early fifties and not a person one would want to irritate. There wasn't a single swimmer on the team who didn't respect and fear the strange old man, who was also fatherly and safe in his own way.

"Three laps around the baseball court and then hit the showers," the coach roared as he went inside the swimming hall carrying a big bag full of equipment for practice.

"Yeah, nice to see you, too," Rick muttered as the boys started to run.

"Catch me if you can!" Alex shouted to his friend and sprinted with all the power that a sixteen-year-old jock had in his muscles. His body was in good shape thanks to hundreds of training sessions. Rick didn't have a chance.

After the first lap, Alex slowed down and waited until Rick reached him. The boys, who had been best friends since the first grade, ran the second lap together.

"Why is it taking so long? I wonder if Sam managed to get the beer," Rick panted.

"Jeez. Will you stop worrying already? Sam knows how to convince Maggie," Alex said.

"Good old Maggie, the one we can always trust," Rick said with a smirk. Alex felt another wave of guilt as he smiled back at his friend.

Speak of the devil; Sam entered the baseball stadium and joined Alex and Rick. He was grinning widely, and the other boys knew the mission had been accomplished.

"Party on Friday!" Sam shouted so loudly that, had the stadium been full, everybody in the stands would have heard the good news.

Alex looked at his friend and smiled again. The trio had gone through several practices and training camps together, and they had become best buddies. If baseball players were the alpha males in the high school social hierarchy, these three swimmers stood firmly on the second podium. Besides, they were better looking than the baseball players for sure, which made them more popular among the girls. Alex didn't want to admit it, but he enjoyed his popularity. Shallow or not, it felt good and fostered his self-esteem. He was proud of his athletic achievements and his friends on the swim team.

"Summer vacation is way too short," Sam complained as they were about to finish their last lap.

"No shit," Rick agreed. "I wish this were already the last year."

The lack of interest in their studies amused Alex. While the three of them were juniors, some of Alex's closest friends on the team were already seniors, planning their futures at reputable colleges. Alex wanted to follow their example, if for no other reason than to make his parents satisfied.

Alex's mother was a lawyer who had high expectations for her son's academic career. Luckily, Alex showed some interest in studying law. Had he been planning for a career at the local Burger King, like Sam, his mother would have kicked his lazy ass out of the house already. Sara Wesley had high standards for her son.

The boys jogged back to the swimming hall and changed their sweaty clothes in the locker room. Soon, Coach Hanson entered and checked that all his athletes were present.

"Okay, guys. We have a two-hour practice today. We start in ten," Coach Hanson shouted. "No speedos in the showers. I want to keep my pool clean," he added and left.

Following the order, Alex hung his trunks on the rack, stood under the first free shower and felt the refreshing water stream down his sweaty back. As he had done hundreds of times before, he soaped his body and let the water rinse him clean. Then he got dressed in his red speedo and headed for the pool. The others followed him obediently.

The coach didn't spare his whistle, and the boys swam back and forth down the fifty-meter lane more times than any of them could count. After two hours and fifteen minutes, the group of exhausted but happy teenagers climbed from the pool. The practice had been successful, and Coach Hanson had even said some encouraging words. Alex beamed because he had just broken his old record in the two-hundred-meter freestyle.

"Wanna play some *Call of Duty*?" Rick asked Alex when they were washing themselves in the showers.

"Absolutely! You are so dead already," Alex replied confidently and pushed Rick's arm.

Almost as much as he loved swimming, Alex enjoyed playing video games with his best friend. The Donovans had spent three weeks traveling the country during the summer, and Alex was happy Rick was back.

They finished their showers and agreed to meet at Rick's house in an hour. Alex looked at his watch and realized dinner would probably be ready soon. His mother was a better lawyer than a cook, but she did her best to gather the family together every evening. It wasn't a big family; Alex was the only child of Paul and Sara Wesley.

"See you soon!" Alex said to his friend and left the dressing room.

He was opening the front door of his Mustang when he heard Sam running toward him. "Hey Alex, um…I don't have enough room for all these. Could you take some of the beers and keep them in your fridge until Friday?" Sam asked, offering a plastic bag to Alex.

"Huh?" Alex replied uneasily. "I can't." He paused before finally admitting, "My parents would kill me if they found them."

"Oh, okay. No problem, church boy. Later." Sam smirked and walked to his truck.

Alex sighed. He hated to disappoint his friend, but he didn't want to be cut loose from his family. The car, the clothes, and all the other financial support from his parents were too important. If there was something certain in his life, it was that his father would go ballistic if he found Alex bringing beer home.

Besides, his friendship with Sam was a constant source of argument with his parents, who thought of Sam as a bad influence on their son. Alex had always disagreed with his mother on this, but recently, he had started to suspect there was some truth in her motherly instincts. He made a mental note not to admit that to her.

Chapter 2

Liam lay on his bed, thinking about his first week at his new high school. It wasn't easy, it seemed, for a shy sixteen-year-old boy to find new friends. He had met another guy in chemistry class whose situation was similar, and they had ended up doing lab work together. The boy was crazy about ice hockey and miniature airplanes. They didn't seem to share any common interests, and Liam thought they were unlikely to become close friends. Still, it was nice to have someone to work with during class. At least he wasn't completely alone, which was a good starting point.

The best thing about his new school was the blond jock. There was no denying it. Liam thought about his athletic body and felt slightly aroused. *How can somebody be so cute and so unreachable at the same time?* He sighed but couldn't help smiling at the image of his dream boy with his well-defined pecs, not too big but just perfect. That, combined with his narrow waist, would have made Liam guess he was a swimmer even without the swim team's t-shirt the boy had worn today.

Liam wasn't much of a sports fan. In his hometown, he had felt quite different from the other boys, who were always competing with each other in sports. He had realized quickly that this lack of interest was something he shared with Matthew, who loved playing Carcassonne with him in the school library. Matthew had also liked to listen, with admiration, when Liam played the piano. Liam had even tried to teach Matthew how to play; after a couple weeks, they agreed it wasn't worth the effort.

Sometimes, Liam watched sports on TV, but it was mostly diving or men's one-hundred meters—and his motive wasn't athletic. He enjoyed watching the young male athletes in their revealing uniforms. Liam imagined how the blond jock would look in his tiny speedo, and his imagination quickly produced the smallest speedo in the history of sports. The suit fit perfectly on the blond boy—his *swimmer boy*.

Just as he started to enjoy this image, jealousy slammed him in the face. The dark-haired girl in the pink sweater—the one who had followed the jock around all week like a puppy trailing its master—must be his girlfriend. The observation was so depressing that Liam closed his eyes and clenched his fists in anger and disappointment. Obviously, he understood there were far too many *ifs* in any scenario in which the jock was gay and in love with Liam. He had been naïve and felt embarrassed.

Liam had been sure he was the only gay in his old high school. His hopes had been higher when he entered Fairmont. Unfortunately, the corridors at the new school hadn't been populated by cute guys wearing signs reading, "I am gay. Please be my boyfriend!" Maybe he was being too impatient. After all, he had spent only one week at his new school. And then there was his obsession with the blond swimmer. Since the swimmer boy was obviously not playing on his team, he decided to start focusing on other guys.

It had been three years earlier when Liam fully realized that he was developing a crush on Matthew. They had been playing soccer at school. It was morning, and the teacher had insisted the sweaty and dirty boys needed to take a shower before their next class. That was when Liam had seen Matthew naked for the first time, and it was a moment he would never forget. He had never told Matthew about his feelings. First, he had been too afraid, and then, Matthew had left.

Matthew hadn't had a girlfriend, which was common enough for boys their age. Liam hadn't dated either, not that he would have wanted a girlfriend. The whole concept of being with a girl had been too scary, never mind being intimate with a girl. At first, he couldn't understand how anybody would feel comfortable doing that. Later, when his schoolmates started to date girls, he had accepted that it was possible, but he still hadn't wanted it.

Coming out to his parents was something Liam had been thinking a lot about ever since Matthew disappeared from his life. He was proud to be gay and felt that it was something that made him strong and unique. Still, he was struggling to tell his parents. He was fairly sure they wouldn't kick him out of their home; they were at least that reasonable and open-minded. The reason for not telling them was that he couldn't bear the idea of disappointing them. He was afraid they would see him as weak, or even worse, as a failure.

Should I do it now? Liam wondered as he rose to sit on his bed. The thought of coming out felt right but scary, and he wished he had a fag hag with whom he could talk about his feelings. Too bad that fag hags existed only on television and in romance novels.

He would have called Matthew, but he didn't know his number. Liam wasn't sure what Matthew would have said upon hearing the news. They had never talked about gay people, but now it would have felt safer to talk about it when they would not be sitting face to face. If Matthew's reaction was negative, Liam could simply hang up the phone.

Mom, I am gay. Liam repeated the line in his mind. He was nervous and had been pacing in front of his window for over half an hour. *It's now or never*, Liam decided finally and walked to the kitchen, where his mother was cooking dinner.

"Mom, I need to talk with you," he started timidly.

"What does my baby have on his mind?" she asked, not noticing the unusual tone in her son's voice.

"Mom, I am…" Liam started, but he swallowed the most significant part of the well-practiced sentence. "I am going shopping tomorrow, and I need some money for new clothes," he said quickly, feeling both relieved and disappointed.

The big moment was over, and there was no way Liam could turn the conversation back onto its intended track. *What a loser*, he thought as he walked back to his room with the bills that his mother had generously given him.

Liam remembered having the same feeling on an earlier occasion when he had spent a whole afternoon wondering how to tell Matthew about his feelings. He had even arranged the meeples in their Carcassonne game to resemble gay couples, but the wooden characters standing hand-in-hand on the game board had apparently not been a clear-enough hint. One could hardly blame Matthew for not understanding such a lame message.

Maybe it's better that I didn't tell her, Liam thought and sat on his bed. There were so many internet horror stories about teenagers coming out to their parents. Still, he couldn't help feeling cowardly, and his eyes were getting moist. Life was sometimes so unfair.

Undoubtedly, there was no one he could tell at school, but it would have been nice to talk to somebody. A few minutes ago, he had thought that someone could be his mother, but now he decided it would be better to delay telling his parents until he had moved away from home. Keeping the secret for a few more years would be a heavy feeling. Even though the shopping trip had been a lame excuse, Liam decided to buy some new clothes tomorrow after all. Maybe that would cheer him up.

Half an hour later, Liam's mother came to his bedroom, totally unaware of what her son was going through. "Dinner is ready," she said cheerfully. "I tried a new pasta recipe that I saw in a magazine."

Liam smiled at his mother. "Thanks, Mom. I'm super hungry, and it smells delicious," he said. Until he said it, he hadn't realized how hungry he was.

Jenny Green was an excellent cook, and this wasn't just the biased opinion of her husband, Matt—all their friends and relatives happily accepted dinner invitations to their home. Tonight's meal was no exception. Roasted chicken, blue cheese, and pineapple made a perfect companion to penne paste and pepper cream sauce, not to mention the freshly-baked garlic bread, which was beyond delicious.

"How was your first week at school?" Liam's father asked.

His mother followed this with a series of questions. "Did you get a lot of homework? Were the teachers nice? Did you make new friends?"

"And, were there any nice girls?" his father asked, grinning at Liam. "Have I told you that I met your mother in high school?"

"Yes, darling. You've shared that story plenty of times," Liam's mother interrupted.

"My week was good. I didn't get too much homework, and the teachers were okay, too. I also found a partner for chemistry class," Liam answered.

He hoped his father wouldn't notice the missing answer to his question about girls and was relieved when his father focused his attention on his wife instead. Liam listened while they went through their schedules for the next workweek. Their new home still lacked some items, and they agreed to visit the mall on Wednesday.

Mr. Green was a salesman for Locke Diagnostics, a global company that produced medical analyzers and other equipment. He traveled a lot but typically took only domestic trips, which meant he spent most of his nights at home.

Liam considered his father to be a fair and decent person. He had played baseball in high school but was aware of Liam's lack of interest in sports and had encouraged him to take piano lessons. Liam was grateful he didn't live in a family of sports lunatics.

Why can't I tell them? Liam moaned to himself as he ate the last pieces of his dinner. The pasta was delicious, but his incapability to open up to his parents was agonizing. It was tearing him apart, and he felt he might start crying again. It was hard to swallow the pasta and his tears at the same time.

"Something wrong, honey?" his mother asked, obviously aware that her son wasn't okay. Liam swallowed again and waited long enough to make sure his voice wouldn't crack.

"No, Mom. I'm just tired. First week at a new school and all," Liam answered.

"Oh, I see," his mother said and started to collect the dishes to put them in the dishwasher.

Liam realized his second chance to come out had just passed, and he returned to his room and took his PlayStation from the last unopened moving box. He connected the HDMI cable to his television and was delighted to notice the wireless controller still had some power left. For a moment, he browsed his collection of games until he found the one he was looking for. A moment later, the machine gun of Sergeant John MacTavish was singing its deadly song.

Several hours later, Liam felt both relaxed and tired. He hadn't realized how exhausted he was until it became impossible to shoot enemies because his eyes wouldn't stay open. He remembered a night he had spent at Matthew's home when they had been sitting next to each other, watching some boring movie. At some point, Liam woke up and noticed Matthew had fallen asleep and was leaning against him. The boy felt warm, and Liam could barely resist the temptation to stroke his hair. He did not, however, and the next time he woke up, Matthew was no longer in the room.

Damn. It's two o'clock on Saturday morning, Liam thought when he saw the clock on his wall. He turned off the console and walked to the window to draw the curtains. Then he saw two boys, about his age, walking down the street. The light from the street lamps was dim, but Liam was sure the boys were holding each other. One guy was resting his head against the other's shoulder.

A young gay couple! This cannot be happening, Liam thought. Astonished, he stared at the guys and recognized one of them. It was Sam, the rebel whose late arrival he had witnessed in his very first class. Sam had displayed the same "fuck the world" attitude throughout the week.

Sam couldn't be gay, Liam concluded. He wasn't. When the boys came out of the shadows, Liam saw that Sam was heavily drunk and could hardly walk. The other boy was doing his best to keep Sam standing. *Good to have friends who will take you home*, Liam said to himself, though he didn't think too highly of Sam. The guy was a bully and a loser.

Maybe, in Fairmont, the idea of a young gay couple walking hand-in-hand was quite unrealistic after all, Liam thought as he got into bed. Life felt unfair. A boy and a girl could walk everywhere as a couple, but he couldn't walk hand-in-hand with his boyfriend. Not that he had one. Then his mind returned to the blond swimmer boy, and all of a sudden, the world was beautiful again.

Chapter 3

"We're having a party tonight!" Rick shouted, and the other guys washing themselves in the shower room joined in his excitement.

Alex, who had stopped to talk to Coach Hanson, entered the room and took the shower next to Rick. He pressed the button casually and felt the warm water begin to massage his tired muscles.

"I assume you're taking your girl to the party," Rick said, smiling at Alex.

"Who are you talking about?" Alex said, playing oblivious.

"Dude! The whole school knows Sofia is drooling over you," Rick said. He poked Alex on the shoulder. "Don't be a dumb jock; I'm not buying it. You'd better taste the meat before it gets cold."

Alex rolled his eyes. He and Sofia had known each other for years, ever since Sofia and her family moved to Fairmont. They hadn't been close until last spring, when she had taken the initiative to get to know Alex better. She was a pretty girl who had been surrounded by a lot of horny jocks, but she had made it clear that she wasn't interested in them. Eventually, they had noticed the connection between Alex and Sofia and had dropped their interest.

Everybody was waiting for the couple to start dating, but so far, it hadn't happened. For months, Alex had felt pressure from Rick to make a move.

"Yeah, she is kind of sexy," Alex finally said, smirking.

Even though he didn't fully agree with the other boys' constant praise of her looks, Sofia's interest in him flattered Alex. On the other hand, Sofia was rather impulsive and short-tempered, which made her even scary at times. Sam quickly joined the discussion and thoroughly analyzed every part of Sofia's body. His detailed and blunt description of Sofia's valleys and hills made Alex uncomfortable, and he blushed slightly.

"You'd better stop before you get boners!" Rick shouted from the other side of the room.

Patrick, a senior and a year older than the others, turned to look at him. "Stop staring at my dick, homo," he said and laughed.

Rick didn't get the joke and gave him an angry gaze. "There are no faggots on this team," he said, emphasizing each word, and total silence settled in the room for a moment.

"So, Alex has this hot chick. What about the rest of you?" Patrick asked, knowing very well the others were involuntarily single. Patrick was dating another senior, and their relationship seemed serious.

Rick and Sam were silent, thinking of how to reply to Patrick's comment about their lack of girlfriends.

"I guess I need to ask if Sofia wants to go," Alex said, in an effort to stop the uneasy silence. Then the topic had passed, and the boys started talking about swim practice.

Patrick had just improved his individual record in the one-hundred-meter medley. Still, it was Alex who was the unquestionable star of the team and had won the most swimming competitions during his high school career. Coach Hanson believed strongly in Alex's chances of winning a medal in the next national championships, which would guarantee him an athletic scholarship to any college.

The coach was proud of him, and his teammates encouraged and supported him, even though it meant less attention on them. But no matter how much the coach and Alex's friends cheered him, his biggest and most fanatical cheerleader was his father—not that anybody in his right mind would call Paul Wesley a cheerleader. The man was anything but pretty and flexible.

Thirty years and eighty pounds ago, Mr. Wesley had been a decent high school boxer. Unfortunately, the short-tempered boy had been unable to keep his fists away from fights outside the ropes, and his promising career had ended. The sentence was only probationary, but in his rigorous Catholic school, it had been a serious black mark. Mrs. Wesley believed her husband was re-living his athletic career through his son.

Alex felt lucky that his father was so eager to pay for all his training equipment, gym membership, and training camp costs. Despite how busy his father was at work, Alex couldn't remember a competition during which his father hadn't been watching and cheering from the stands. Thanks to sports, there had always been a strong connection between father and son. Recently, however, Alex had started to feel that something unexplainable was pushing them farther and farther apart.

Alex, Rick, Sam, and Patrick left the swimming hall and drove to a park near their houses. Fairmont wasn't a big town, and the boys knew they could walk home if nobody was in a condition to drive after the party. A couple of their friends from the swimming team had joined them, as had Patrick's girlfriend.

"I called Sofia. She and Rosa are coming soon," Rick announced to Alex.

"Thanks, bro," Alex said sarcastically, not sure whether to be happy about his friend's efforts to pair him with Sofia. Rosa was Sofia's best friend and went to Fairmont High as well.

Twenty minutes later, Sofia and Rosa arrived, and Sofia's face beamed when she saw Alex. "Hi, darling," she said to Alex as sweetly as she could. She was obviously putting on a show for her friends, earmarking Alex for herself.

"Rick, would you get Rosa something to drink?" Sofia said, organizing company for her friend.

"Anything, milady," Rick said to Rosa.

It was a warm evening, and a light breeze was blowing from the south. The sky was clear while the sunset made the horizon glow yellow and red. The idyllic beauty of the moment was counterbalanced by the fact that the teens were getting wasted.

It didn't take long before Sam was laying on the grass and puking up his lunch. The seniors laughed at him, telling him he should practice more. Alex disagreed. He wished Sam would drink less, but he didn't believe it would happen.

The early autumn darkness became deeper and deeper, and Alex and Patrick decided to build a fire. They had collected wood earlier when it was still bright enough to find some in the nearby forest. Sitting around the flames, the teens drank the evening away.

"I fucking love this park," Sam stammered sometime around midnight. He curled up in the warmth of the campfire—five minutes later, he was snoring.

"Maybe we should've asked Coach Hanson to the party," one of the seniors said as a joke, and the whole group laughed.

"Okay, boys, I will teach you how real men drink beer," said another senior, imitating the coach.

"We ain't no fairies!" Rick shouted and raised his bottle. Alex scowled at his friend but said nothing because the other guys started to cheer.

Half an hour later, the jocks got tired of ranting about the hard time the coach gave them in practices.

Alex took another beer from the bag. Actually, it was only his second, but he didn't want the others to notice he wasn't keeping up with their pace. He sat on a stone close to the fire, and Sofia immediately joined him.

Rick and Rosa found a place for themselves a little farther from the campfire. Alex watched how Rick took Rosa into his lap and stroked her hair. *The horndog is definitely falling for Rosa*, Alex thought but couldn't remember Rick showing any interest in Rosa at school. Maybe his friend was just too shy to do so.

Alex saw them kiss, and they looked like they were trying to eat each other. *Definitely not too shy*, he thought, smiling to himself.

"Do you like me?" Sofia asked out of the blue.

"Um…yes," Alex stammered and felt himself blushing.

"I like you, too," she confessed.

She moved her face close to his and stared at Alex with her big, beautiful eyes. Her smile was sweet and irresistible, and then their lips touched. Alex was tense and felt clumsy. He didn't know what he should do next, but it felt oddly good to kiss. Just as he started to relax, he felt Sofia's hand on his leg, moving toward his crotch.

"What's happening here?" Sam shouted, staggering toward the stone where Alex and Sofia were sitting. He had finally woken up, and his clothes were dirty from sleeping on the grass.

"I hope I'm not interrupting anything," Sam continued.

He sat between the lovebirds, ignoring Sofia, who looked beyond angry. Alex took his cell phone from his pocket to check the time.

"Don't worry, you didn't interrupt anything," he said. "Besides, it's late. I'd better go home."

Alex caught Patrick's eye, indicating he wanted to talk with him privately. He left Sofia sitting on the rock and met Patrick just out of hearing distance of the others. "I'm worried about Sam," he said when they were alone.

"Me too," Patrick said. "But don't worry about it. I'll make sure he gets home."

"Thanks, I hoped you would," Alex said and patted Patrick on his shoulder. Patrick was always the one he could trust.

"I'm not going anywhere," Sam said, slurring his words when Patrick offered his hand to pull Sam up.

"Yes, you are," Patrick replied, indisputably.

Patrick took decisive hold of the drunken boy and led him from the park. Sam had no choice but to follow. Alex felt grateful that his friend was in good hands.

"I need to pee," Rick announced to everybody.

"Need me to hold it?" joked a senior, who was amused with Rick's announcement.

"Keep your faggy little fingers off my dick, homo," Rick answered.

Looking annoyed, Rick marched behind the bushes to empty his bladder. When he came back, he kissed Rosa as if to prove something to the other boys. Nobody paid attention.

"Will you walk me home?" Sofia asked Alex. She was clearly disappointed that Alex was leaving but did her best not to show it.

"Um, sure," Alex replied, trying to hide his intention to walk alone. Happily, she took Alex's hand, and they began to walk toward the center of Fairmont.

It was a silent night. Alex could hear only the occasional sounds of distant cars while he was thinking of Sam. They had been friends for years, but Alex had started to have concerns about their friendship. Sam was regularly late to classes and hardly did any of his homework. Still, it was his badass behavior that disturbed Alex the most.

"Thinking of something?" Sofia asked.

Alex had been silent since they left the park. "Just worried about Sam," he said without elaborating.

"Don't worry. Patrick will take him home," she reassured.

"Yes, he will," Alex said, and they continued walking on in silence.

Fifteen minutes later, they arrived at Sofia's house. They stopped and looked at each other. It was again a moment when Alex didn't know what to say.

"Goodnight," he said finally, in a soft voice, which caused Sofia to roll her eyes.

"You're not going to give me a goodnight kiss, are you?" she asked, smiling innocently.

Alex did what was asked and then walked Sofia to the front door. They kissed one more time before Sofia went in.

"Where the hell have you been?" Paul Wesley roared when Alex opened the front door five minutes later.

Alex winced with fear at his father's tone. He switched on the lights and saw his. father standing in pajama pants in the hall. He didn't look happy.

"I…I was in the park with a couple of friends," Alex answered, unsure how his father would take it.

It didn't go over well, but before his father could unleash the next wave of his anger, his mother walked into the hall.

"Alex, we haven't agreed that you can come home after midnight," she said with a disapproving look, "and I don't like you spending time with those boys. You were with them, weren't you?"

Alex knew she was referring to Sam and didn't know what to say. "Sorry, Mom," he said, feeling defeated.

His father took a couple of steps closer but looked a little calmer. Most likely, this was because of his wife's appearance. "Have you been drinking?" he asked, staring relentlessly at his son.

"No, Dad, of course not," Alex lied quickly.

The look on his father's face became milder. "My boy. I knew I could trust you," he said with a pinch of pride in his voice. Alex felt his conscience tugging at him as he smiled cautiously at his parents.

"Okay, let's go to bed," his father said, and the crisis in the hall was over.

Alex was relieved. His father was hot-headed. Though he normally calmed down pretty quickly, this incident had been unusually short. Alex had been lucky this time and made a mental note not to push his luck again any time soon.

When Alex was a baby, his father had hit his mother as a result of some stupid argument. Thanks to plenty of therapy sessions in which his father had "volunteered" to participate, Alex's parents were still together. Maybe the newborn Alex also had something to do with his mother's decision not to leave her husband. Whatever the case, Alex's father knew he couldn't repeat that mistake ever again.

Rolling in his bed, Alex heard the echo of his mother's words: "I don't like you spending time with those boys."

Who is she to decide my friends? Alex was tired of his parents always believing they knew what was best for him. Without an academic degree, his mother would never give him her full approval, and it was evident that his father's dream was for Alex to become an Olympic champion or something.

Why isn't it enough to just be me? Alex thought, feeling the pressure of his parents' expectations.

His thoughts moved to Rick. It was now evident that Rosa had taken an interest in Rick, and it seemed mutual. Alex felt jealous and feared his friend might have less time to play video games with him. Also, he was worried that his friendship with Sam was starting to fall apart. Why couldn't everything just stay as it was for a moment so Alex could enjoy what he had?

Finally, the sound of Alex's light snoring filled his bedroom. In Sofia's bedroom, half a mile away, a pink pen was smoking as she wrote about Alex in her diary.

Chapter 4

It was raining, as it often did in Fairmont at the end of October. The hot days of late summer were over, and nature was preparing for winter. Many trees had already lost their leaves, and the ones still hanging on were colored yellow and red. Liam held his umbrella with both hands, fighting against the wind. Just as he arrived in the schoolyard, the first bell rang, calling the students to start a new week of school.

Liam walked to the school alone, as he had done throughout his nine weeks in Fairmont. Part of him liked the solitude because it gave him time to think, and his young mind, indeed, was full of thoughts. Still, he missed Matthew and those mornings when they had met in front of Matthew's home and walked to school together. Unlike Liam, who hated early mornings, Matthew had always been full of energy.

The door to the history classroom was locked, and Liam waited in the corridor with the other students. To his big surprise, he saw Sam walking by the lockers.

Wow, he's early today, Liam thought and couldn't help checking the jock's body. He didn't like Sam, but he had to admit the jock was easy on eyes. His shirt was tight enough to reveal his muscles and the bulge in his jeans was worth another glance. Their eyes met; Sam's were full of annoyance. Liam hid his smile and turned his head away quickly.

Before Sam could do or say anything else, Mr. Timothy arrived and opened the door. The students meandered into the room as Mr. Timothy switched on the video projector and began to speak. Liam listened carefully while the teacher lectured them on the most significant events of the First World War. It was clear that questions about the subject would appear on the final exam.

As Mr. Timothy wrapped up the topic, Liam felt something hit the back of his neck. He assumed it was a piece of Sam's eraser. Since the jock was too dumb to take any notes during classes, the best way he could think of to use his eraser was to toss it, piece by piece, at Liam. Liam didn't mind Sam doing it, but he was devastated when he glanced back and saw that his dream boy, the blond swimmer, had joined the club. His cute and friendly face was clearly false, Liam decided.

Time was creeping past, and Mr. Timothy went on and on. Finally, the bell rang. Liam collected his pencils and notes and put them into his bag. He was close to the door when Sam and his friends rushed out of the room. As he passed, Sam pushed Liam into the doorframe.

"Dude! That must have hurt. You should watch where you're walking!" Sam yelled.

He grinned venomously, and his friends were laughing. Liam looked at the blond swimmer; for a moment, he thought he could see compassion in his face. Then the swimmer followed Sam into the hallway.

Luckily, Liam's next class was chemistry. He had started to like his ice-hockey-maniac lab partner, Jacob, who was pretty cool after all. Jacob wasn't a jock but enjoyed watching sports on TV, and Liam was more than willing to forgive him that handicap. Nobody was perfect, after all, and Jacob behaved decently and didn't throw anything at him.

"What do you like to watch on TV?" Jacob asked after a long story about yesterday's NHL results.

"Well...*Teen Wolf*, for example," Liam said shyly and read his mistake immediately in Jacob's face.

"Oh," Jacob said. After a long pause, he added, "Isn't that kind of...kind of gay or something?"

Liam blushed.

"Sorry, didn't mean to embarrass you," Jacob said and jumped to the next topic, which was ice hockey, of course. Liam decided not to talk to Jacob again about his obsession with the TV series featuring half-naked guys.

Lunchtime finally came, and thanks to a too-light breakfast, Liam's stomach was growling loudly. He scooped an enormous amount of pasta carbonara onto his plate and looked for an empty seat in the dining room, when suddenly, somebody pushed him from behind. Liam and his lunch crashed to the floor, and the whole dining room exploded with laughter.

"Don't you like the pasta? Or do you just prefer eating off the floor?" Sam asked loudly.

Liam was close to tears. To escape the embarrassing situation, he rushed to the restroom. The bacon, eggs, and cream had left marks on his shirt, but he was able to wipe away the solid pieces of food. Fortunately, there was no tomato sauce in the pasta, but one could still read the day's menu on his shirt.

As if the whole situation hadn't been bad enough, the door opened and the blond swimmer entered the restroom. Liam tensed, assuming the jock wanted to push his head into the sink and wet his hair. Liam took hold of the handles near him, but to his surprise, the jock walked to the urinals and unzipped his pants, hardly paying any attention to Liam. When he realized the jock wasn't going to do anything to him, Liam left the restroom quietly.

Feeling hungry but too afraid to return to the dining room, Liam found a hiding place on the staircase that led to the basement. He waited there for the next class to start. Once the bell rang, he wiped away the tears from his eyes and left. Outside, the storm had gotten worse. The drainage system couldn't remove all the water coming from the sky, and the schoolyard flooded.

The day continued, and Liam's next two classes were math and biology. Apparently, the back-seat terrorists had run out of erasers, and Liam didn't feel anything hitting his back. When the class ended, learning from his earlier mistake, he waited to leave until Sam and his friends were gone. The strategy worked, and he was able to avoid another collision with the doorframe.

After his last class, Liam checked the hallway. It was empty, so he assumed it was safe to walk to his locker. When he opened the locker, he heard footsteps behind him and turned immediately, looking scared. A young girl, most likely a freshman, walked by looking at him, puzzled. Liam turned back to his locker, packed his bag, and headed out.

It had stopped raining, but the sky was still dark. Hating the idea of getting wet, Liam hurried across the schoolyard, fearing the rain would start again. Once, when he and Matthew had been wandering in the forest and a storm surprised them, they had tried to find shelter under a big tree but ended up soaked to their skin. Thinking how hot Matthew had looked in his wet clothes brought a little smile to his face.

Just as he walked through the gate and turned toward home, he heard someone speaking behind him.

"Well, well…where are you going, pansy boy?" It was Sam.

Liam turned. Across the yard, he saw Sam and his friends, the blond swimmer and the other dark-haired jock. Liam started walking again, faster, and he heard the boys follow him. He turned left at the next intersection and began to run, but his pursuers ran after him.

Liam had a good head start, but he knew he couldn't outrun the jocks. He had to find a place to hide, and he had to find it before they got too close. He saw an abandoned gas station and ran behind it. Unfortunately, it was a dead end. The building and a tall fence blocked his escape. He looked desperately for a door or a hole in the fence, but there were none.

Liam spotted a large trashcan in the corner and crouched behind it. Seconds later, the jocks appeared at a run. "Are you sure you saw him come back here?" the black-haired boy asked.

"No, but where else he could be?" Sam answered.

The blond swimmer walked toward the trashcan and opened the cover. Liam held his breath and felt the first raindrops in his hair. He was sure they would discover him any second.

"Shit, what a smell." The blond swimmer dropped the cover and took a couple of steps back. "Why are we chasing him? Let's leave before the rain gets heavier."

Sam looked around one more time and agreed.

After the jocks left, Liam waited another fifteen minutes before he dared to emerge from his hiding place. *What a perfect day*, he thought sarcastically when he finally saw his house. He was soaked, tired, and annoyed.

"Okay, guys, that's it. Let's finish up. Tomorrow we start at half-past four!" Coach Hanson shouted, and the jocks hit the showers. Alex took the shower next to Patrick.

"Have you decided which colleges you're going to apply to?" Patrick asked.

"Yeah, I've got a couple in mind," Alex answered. He explained his plans to Patrick, who listened carefully.

Patrick was more or less the only guy on the team Alex could talk to about his academic aspirations, which bothered him. He knew that graduating from high school would be an achievement in itself for Sam, but he had hoped to go to the same college with Rick, at least. Sadly, Rick hadn't shown much interest in college so far.

Alex agreed to have pizza with Patrick and his girlfriend that weekend. Then he said goodbye to Rick, who was dressing in a hurry as he had a weekly family dinner with his parents. Alex assumed Rick's workaholic father wanted to make amends for his absence by taking his family to dinner once a week.

"Alex, I need to talk to you," Sam said in a serious tone.

Alex, who had just removed his speedo and was looking for a fresh pair of boxers in his sports bag, stopped and turned around. He gave Sam a questioning look, but Sam gestured to him to get dressed before he continued the conversation.

"Am I decent enough now?" Alex joked once he had put on his boxers, socks, and a t-shirt.

"Fine," Sam muttered and continued in a louder voice, "Could you loan me some money?" He looked embarrassed; apparently, it didn't suit his badass reputation to ask for help.

"How much?" Alex said, taking a twenty-dollar bill from his wallet.

"One-thousand, five-hundred dollars," Sam replied casually.

"Wow," Alex said, putting the bill back into his wallet. "I don't have that much money. Why do you need it?"

Sam looked somber. "It's better that you don't know."

Alex tried to fish for more information, but Sam kept quiet. *Let's hope he's not involved in anything criminal,* Alex thought as they left the swimming hall together.

After the heavy rain on Monday, Wednesday evening looked much better. It was dry, and the sun had been shining the whole day. It was rather cold, which wasn't surprising, given the season.

Sam smirked suddenly. "You should've seen the face of that pansy boy when I met him today in the cafeteria," he said.

Alex sighed. "You didn't push his lunch to the floor again, did you?" he asked.

"Unfortunately not, the principal was there," Sam replied, annoyed. "The old man won't always be standing there, though. I'll get my chance."

And he will get his chance, Alex thought. *Probably tomorrow, and on how many more days?*

"Why are we bullying that…pansy boy?" Alex finally asked.

Sam stopped walking and glared at Alex. "Haven't you seen how he stares at us? Why are you defending him? Don't tell me you're a cocksucker, too," he said.

"I'm not defending anybody, and I don't even know him. I was just asking," Alex said, feeling irritated. "I need to go. Sofia is probably waiting for me."

Alex drove from the parking lot, almost hitting another car at the entrance, and turned toward his home. Sam was always playing his games with the smaller guys.

For the second time this week, Alex was disappointed that Rick wasn't there to play video games with him: first, the date with Rosa and now the family dinner. Maybe he could invite Rick and Rosa to do something with him and Sofia that weekend.

"How was swimming practice?" Alex's father asked him at the dinner table. Alex gave a short summary of the practice to his father, who looked at him proudly.

"That's my son," he said, and he started to talk about his own achievements as a high school boxer twenty-five years ago. Alex and his mother looked at each other. This was a story they had heard many times before.

Once dinner was over, Alex thought about visiting Sofia but offered instead to help his mother clean the table and wash the dishes.

"Have you thought about what I said to you about Sam? I don't like you spending time with him," Alex's mother said after his father had left the kitchen. Alex sighed. Of course, his mother wouldn't drop the topic easily.

"Yes, yes," Alex said, sounding irritated. He didn't like his mother intervening in his life.

His mother heard his tone and said calmly, "Alex, I am just worried about you. Even though it sounds cliché, you have your whole life in front of you. I don't want you to spoil it."

Alex rolled his eyes but couldn't fully disagree, bSam had always been like his missing brother. When his super-health-obsessed mother had equipped him with vegetables and muesli bars for their training camp, Sam had immediately volunteered to share his chips and candy, which they had had to eat on the sly. Like Alex's mother, Coach Hanson couldn't understand the importance of sugar, fat, and salt in the boys' diets.

Alex started to do his homework, but his thoughts shifted to Sam. He couldn't understand why Sam needed fifteen-hundred dollars. Even though Alex's parents were pretty wealthy, Sam knew that Alex himself didn't have that much money. The more he thought about the episode in the swimming hall locker room, the more convinced he became that Sam was in some sort of trouble.

He wanted to help his friend, but he knew he couldn't ask his mother to give him the money. She would certainly want to know why he needed it, and he couldn't tell her it was for Sam. It was frustrating. Sam had also made it very clear that he didn't want Alex to know the reason for the money. Alex couldn't find a way to help his friend, so he decided to do nothing, at least for the time being.

Chapter 5

Liam woke up and crawled out of his bed. He could feel, even in his room, that the weather outside was freezing. It had been snowing all night, which was expected since it was already December. He smiled as he saw his bed hair in the mirror. *I definitely need a shower.*

His expression became serious when he recalled the recent events at school. Liam had learned to wait until one of the teachers entered the cafeteria before getting his lunch. Even Sam wasn't stupid enough to try something when adults were present, and most of the time, Liam was able to eat his lunch from the plate instead of the cafeteria floor.

However, Sam had innovated new ways to torment Liam. One day, he had gotten his chance to push Liam's head into a sink and turn on the cold water. After that, Liam had avoided the bathrooms, even when his bladder was about to burst. It was humiliating to run home with his legs crossed, but it kept his hair dry.

Liam picked up the new vanilla shampoo his mother had bought and began to wash his hair. The hot water felt so comfortable, and soon all the glass surfaces in the bathroom were covered with steam. He rubbed soap on his body and thought about the blond jock, which caused his erection to start to grow.

Twenty minutes later, his teeth were brushed and his hair was perfect. It was time for one final check of his bag to make sure he had packed all the books he needed.

As he was leaving, his mother shouted from the kitchen, "Honey! Are you not going to eat anything?"

"I'm not hungry," he replied as he shut the door. It was going to be a long day at school because of some extra classes, and he was worried that, if he ate too much, he wouldn't make it without a bathroom break.

I'm an idiot, Liam thought as he headed through the blizzard toward the school. He couldn't understand why he was so obsessed with the blond swimmer boy. Despite his divine appearance, the jock was an idiot, whose gang got satisfaction out of bullying Liam.

Speaking of the devil, he saw Sam, the blond swimmer boy, and their dark-haired friend walking from the parking area toward the main gate of the school. Liam's first thought was to run to the schoolyard before the jocks saw him. It was unlikely to work, but maybe he would be hidden by the snowfall.

But it was too late. "Well, hello there, pansy boy! How are you?" Sam yelled in a mocking tone.

"I'm fine. Thanks for asking, tiny boy," Liam answered. "Unfortunately, my schedule is full today."

Liam was tired of the gang constantly bullying him; still, he wasn't sure where he was finding the courage to confront Sam in front of his friends. Surprised by the answer, Sam stopped walking.

"What do you mean?" Sam asked, looking confused.

"I appreciate your money, but like I said, I don't have time to suck your tiny dick today. I'm fully booked. Sorry," Liam said with a regretful expression on his face as he could.

The blond swimmer and his friend burst into laughter. Sam didn't. His face turned red with anger.

Sam stepped to Liam and grabbed his jacket. He dragged the small boy to the snowbank on the side of the road and pushed him into it. Sam had lost the verbal battle but wanted to make his physical dominance very clear. Luckily, he didn't make any more of a scene in front of the school than he already had. Instead, he marched to the schoolyard. "Fucking faggot," were the last words Liam heard him say.

Liam was lying in the snow. The blond swimmer kept looking at him, and his expression was serious. For a moment, Liam thought he would retaliate on behalf of his friend, but he didn't. On the contrary, he was almost smiling as Liam rose from the snow and brushed off his clothes. Finally, the blond swimmer and his friend turned to follow Sam, who had already disappeared into the yard.

The rest of the school day was startlingly uneventful. Liam saw Sam a couple of times during the day, and the tight look in his eyes made it clear the war was far from over. If he knew Sam at all, it had just started. Liam was worried about the jock's next move, but he had decided it was time to start fighting back.

The sun was setting, and long, dark shadows surrounded the Fairmont High School campus. Alex pulled the zipper of his coat higher and kept hiding behind a snow-covered bush that grew by the main entrance of the swimming hall. A hundred-and-fifty yards from him, Sam was talking to two suspicious-looking older men.

Alex was worried. After the incident with the new guy in front of the school that morning, Sam had been behaving strangely. Alex had to admit that the small kid's courage had surprised him, but he was worried about what Sam's next move would be.

Sam and the older men were too far away for Alex to overhear their conversation. It looked like they were arguing about something before one of the men pushed Sam on the chest. The other man pulled his friend back, placing himself between them to calm the situation, preventing a potential fight.

The first man looked frustrated and started to walk away. His friend pointed at Sam, and then he left, too. Alex watched Sam wait for several minutes before walking to his truck.

What the heck is going on? Alex thought. He saw Sam pull out of the parking lot and heard his mother's warning in his head: *"Think about your future. Sam isn't good company for you."*

Alex drove home and started on his homework. An hour later, Sofia called him, but Alex was too worried about Sam to answer. He picked up his phone and read the text message that Rick had sent him the previous day: "Is Sam in trouble? He asked me for money but didn't say why."

At half-past eight, Alex decided to drive to city hall to see the opening of the Christmas market. He wanted to watch as the Christmas lights were switched on and hoped to meet some of his friends there. Alex liked Christmas; he liked all the lights, food, decorations, and atmosphere. But, more than anything, he wanted something to think about other than Sam.

He had driven less than a mile when he saw Sam's truck. With a heavy sigh, he decided to follow his friend. He had a hard time keeping the truck in sight; it was speeding aggressively and swerving from side to side. Within five minutes, Alex no longer knew where Sam was. It started to snow again, which made chasing his friend even harder.

Alex drove here and there for twenty minutes before finally giving up. He cursed. If Sam was stupid enough not to let him help, why should Alex try to force his help onto him? Sam was stubborn. He had always been.

The snowfall became thicker as Alex turned back toward the center of Fairmont. He was passing a gas station when he hit the brakes. His car skidded on the slippery road before stopping. Sam was carrying something in the lot of the gas station, and he was clearly drunk.

"What the fuck are you doing?" Alex cried in amazement when he saw Sam carrying a cash register to his truck.

"I'm a rich boy now," Sam slurred and put the cash register in the back seat.

"Are you crazy? Seriously. You can't steal that," Alex said.

"Screw you, rich boy," Sam replied and got into the driver's seat.

Alex ran around the truck, pulled the passenger door open, and jumped in next to Sam. "You're not going anywhere before we talk!" he shouted.

"There's nothing to talk about, pretty boy," Sam snapped. "You've got rich parents, good grades in every fucking class, and a hot chick."

"Um…" was all Alex was able to say. Was Sam jealous of him? "Listen, let's—" he began, but then they heard police sirens. Soon, flashing blue lights illuminated the night.

"Shit, cops," the jocks said at the same time.

Before Alex could do anything, Sam started the engine and hit the gas. The black SUV attacked the snowy road, and Sam could barely keep it on track.

"Fuck! What are you doing? Stop!" Alex cried in vain as the massive truck accelerated toward the city center.

"Can you at least explain why you robbed the gas station?" Alex asked when he realized that Sam wouldn't stop.

"I need money," Sam said, as if it explained everything.

"Yeah, that's a fucking good reason," Alex said.

Sam looked at his friend and sighed. The boys could still hear the sirens, and they saw the lights of a police car in the back mirror.

"Look, Alex, I got problems with my buyer, so I had to borrow money from the Grimm brothers to pay my dealer for the stuff," Sam said.

"What buyer and what stuff and what dealer?" Alex asked. Then he realized what Sam meant. "Oh, please…are you fucking nuts? Loan money from the Grimms!"

"Like I had a choice!" Sam shouted back.

Then Sam saw something. Here and there, people were walking along the road toward the town center, and Liam was among them. He was walking on the road's shoulder, his back facing them.

"The pansy boy!" Sam cried out cheerfully and turned the wheel.

"What? You're not seriously about to drive over him?" Alex said in a panic.

"Why not?" Sam said. "I didn't like him in the first place." He pressed the gas pedal.

As they got closer, Alex saw other high-school-aged kids near Liam but couldn't make out their faces. *Shit, this won't end well*, he thought.

The next events happened in slow motion. The vehicle sped toward Liam, who saw it at the very last moment and tried to jump before it hit him. At the same time, Alex pulled the wheel to change its course while Sam was laughing hysterically. The truck hit something, and Alex felt how it turned around. It skidded a good distance before a lamppost stopped it.

One-hundred feet from the truck, Liam was lying on the ground. His head was bleeding, and his eyes were closed. He didn't witness the arrival of the police officers or see them arrest Sam. Nor did he see the ambulance, which arrived some minutes later.

The evening was dark, and the snowfall soon covered the marks of the collision in which a young high school student lost his life. Soon it would be Christmas, and far away, the Christmas lights of Fairmont's City Hall were twinkling merrily.

Chapter 6

It was Saturday, the fifth of January, and Alex's seventeenth birthday. His mother had baked him a big cake, which was quite unusual for her. First and foremost, she was a lawyer, not a housewife, but today, she had made an exception. She hugged her son, who felt so strongly that his sins were finally forgiven that his eyes became moist.

She cut a big slice of the cake and put it on the table in front of him. "Happy birthday, my dear," she said, smiling.

Alex smiled back. "Thanks, Mom."

On that day, almost a month ago, when Alex arrived home in a police car, his father had been furious to see his son with the officers. But that was nothing compared to how furious he had been when he heard that a young high school student had died in the same collision.

Paul Wesley had made it clear that Alex was not to leave the house, except for school and swimming practice, until his seventeenth birthday. No friends were allowed to visit the Wesleys' house, either.

Alex looked at his father, who smiled lightly and wished him a happy birthday. It was the first time he had seen him smile since the crash. Even Christmas Eve had been very silent in the house, and Alex had spent most of the day in his room, playing video games. On Christmas morning, his parents had taken him to church, something Alex couldn't remember them doing ever before.

"I can't eat this much cake! What would Coach Hanson say?" Alex protested but ate it gratefully. It was delicious, and Alex's eyes moistened again when he thought about how much his parents loved him and how lucky he was to still be alive.

"Thanks, Mom. This is so good," he said. A teardrop was falling down her cheek too.

"Alex, I am so thankful I didn't lose you that night," she said and wiped her eyes.

"The court agreed with the prosecutor," Mr. Wesley said, reading from the newspaper. "They found the act to be intentional. Sam will get a long sentence. Most likely three years, at least."

"Alex, I hope you understand…" his mother started but stopped when she saw the sad, pained expression on Alex's face. He still had occasional nightmares about being in the truck with Sam that night.

The police had questioned Alex a couple times, but the prosecutor decided to drop the charges against him. Besides, Alex had helped the police by giving a thorough description of the events, and eventually, his testimony had left Sam behind bars. The legal system had decided that Alex was innocent, but Alex wasn't sure he agreed.

Paul Wesley put down his coffee cup and folded the newspaper. "Alex, you're going to start your senior year soon. You need to think about your future," he said. His tone was exceptionally conciliatorily as he continued, "It would make your mother and me happy if you put more focus on your studies."

"You might be lucky enough to get an athletic scholarship, but you should take care of your grades, too, just in case," his mother added.

Alex looked at both of them and didn't know whether he was more confused or irritated. "But I've got good grades!" he said.

It was true. He was one of the best in his class at math, and he was doing pretty well in physics and chemistry. With a small additional investment, he would be pretty great in most subjects.

His mother patted his back. "We know. We just want the best possible future for our only child," she said. Alex looked down and stared at his hands. *Of course they care about me.*

"We know the death of your schoolmate is still bothering you. Just remember it wasn't your fault," his mother said and looked at her son with sadness and worry in her eyes. Alex sighed heavily.

"Is it okay if I see Rick later today?" he asked cautiously. Since the accident, he had seen his friends only at school.

"We agreed you would be grounded until today," his father replied. Alex was about to say they hadn't "agreed" on anything but decided to keep silent.

"Your punishment is over," his father said, smiling.

"Thanks."

Later in the afternoon, Alex met Rick at Ed's Diner. They sat at the table by the window and ordered big cheeseburgers with chips and drinks. Alex was drinking Diet Coke to compensate for his unhealthy meal.

"Look at you. Like you need to worry about getting fat," Rick said, laughing.

Alex, who was indeed slim, blushed a little. "Can't I have some principles?" he protested.

"So, how is it with Sofia?" Rick asked after they had eaten their burgers. Alex dipped a chip in the mayo and started to eat it. Rick continued, teasing, "Going to spend some time with her today, birthday boy?"

Alex felt uncomfortable. His relationship with Sofia, if there was one, had ended when his parents grounded him. He was sure she hadn't been especially happy to celebrate New Year's Eve without him, and he didn't even know what to think about her.

"Yeah, I guess I'll see her later today," Alex finally replied.

"Remember to lock your bedroom door. You don't want your parents to walk in on you…you know," Rick said. He was perfectly unaware that Alex's relationship with Sofia hadn't reached that level yet.

"I will," Alex replied unenthusiastically.

Rick looked at his watch and jumped. "Shit, I need to run. I promised to meet Rosa at her house. Her parents are still away visiting some relatives," he said and winked. "Maybe we are both going to get lucky today."

"Maybe," Alex said, smiling at his friend's eagerness.

The sun was shining, which was rare at this time of the year. It was freezing outside, and the light snowfall made Fairmont look beautiful. Alex admired the snow-white scenery as he drove Rick back to his home. He looked at his friend and felt a spike of jealousy in his heart. Had Rick been free, Alex would have asked him to hang out and play some video games. That wasn't an option, though, as Rick had made plans with Rosa.

"Be gentle with Sofia," Rick advised when he left Alex's car.

"Yes, sir," Alex muttered, and he rolled his eyes.

It was a short drive from Rick's home to his own, and Alex spent the entire trip thinking about Sofia. She, for sure, still liked him, and she was pretty and popular. Maybe he should ask her on a date—or, even better, on a double date with Rick and Rosa.

When he got home, he thought about calling Sofia but decided to eat some cake first. Then he realized his room was a mess and he had to clean it. After that, he had to make sure he had clean clothes to wear at school the next day. Two hours later, he was still intending to call Sofia, but he couldn't make his finger hit her number in his smartphone. Finally, he decided it was his birthday, and he could do whatever he wanted.

Spending his birthday alone at home didn't sound like the best choice. Alex decided he needed some exercise. He had always felt that he was too slightly built for ice hockey. However, there was a river close to his home that was frozen for several months every winter. The city cleared the snow to form a skating route that was nearly seven miles long and circled the countryside. Alex loved to skate there.

Half an hour later, he was on the ice with his skates. The thick ice rustled under him as he scudded toward the forest, where the river narrowed. He often had his iPod with him, but today he had decided to leave it at home. He wanted to hear the sounds of nature. It was pure and beautiful. The river had always been his place to calm down after arguments with his parents.

Finally, he reached the point where he typically turned back. He took a chocolate bar from his pocket and ate it even though it was a bit frosty. Then he decided to head home as it was getting dark, and there were no streetlights on the route. He had a flashlight with him, but it was easier to skate when one could see the way without it.

On his way home, he thought about what his parents had said about improving his grades. He had to admit that it made sense. Maybe it was because of the fresh air in the forest, but Alex made a decision then that he should have made months ago. He decided to focus on school, which meant he wouldn't have time for girlfriends, at least not yet. Feeling content and free, he was still smiling when he opened the front door of his home.

That Monday, the spring semester started at Fairmont High School. Mr. Timothy, the history teacher, looked more excited than ever when he explained his plan for the class to his students. The topic of the course was the Second World War, and Mr. Timothy wanted the students to work in pairs and prepare a presentation for the class on a given topic. He had already decided on the pairs, but before he disclosed them, he wanted to give some general instructions.

Mr. Timothy was thirty-five years old, and in addition to being a history teacher, he was also the school's vice principal. He typically wore neat jeans, a black polo shirt, and a jacket, and due to his rather formal clothes and bland haircut, he looked older than he was. There was a rumor he was still single.

The students sat silently until Mr. Timothy finished explaining the project. "Everything clear?" he asked and answered a couple of questions.

The class was pretty peaceful now that Sam was gone. Alex hadn't realized until now how much of a disturbance Sam had caused. He scanned the class and wondered who his partner would be.

"Rick and Rosa, you are a team, and your topic is the invasion of Normandy," Mr. Timothy said.

Rick accepted a stack of papers from Mr. Timothy. Alex was disappointed because he would have wanted to prepare the presentation with Rick. His friend, on the other hand, looked very pleased to be paired with Rosa. The couple were looking at each other, totally ignoring everybody else in the classroom.

Sofia put her hand on Alex's shoulder. "Maybe Mr. Timothy has chosen you to be my partner," she whispered softly.

"Sofia, you will work with Jacob," Mr. Timothy said, almost as if he had heard her. She sighed and glared at the teacher, who completely ignored her reaction.

"We still have a couple of pairs left," Mr. Timothy announced, trying to sound dramatic.

Alex tried to remember who still needed a partner, hoping to be paired with someone who would show at least some interest in the work. History wasn't his strongest subject, and he was determined to improve his grade. Hence, he wanted to work with someone who shared the same ambition.

"And finally, the last team will be Alex and Liam," Mr. Timothy said. Alex's face went pale.

Chapter 7

Liam was glowing with satisfaction. He could hardly believe what Mr. Timothy had just said. *Alex will be working with me!*

The topic the teacher had given them was the Paris Peace Treaties, which had formally established peace between the Allies and Bulgaria, Hungary, Italy, Romania, and Finland. To be honest, Liam didn't care what the topic was as long as he could work with the blond swimmer. However, his happiness was evanescent.

"Can I work with Rick instead?" Liam heard Alex ask with some urgency in his voice. Mr. Timothy stopped arranging his papers and looked at Alex.

"Mr. Wesley, is there a particular reason why you cannot work with Mr. Green?" he asked.

"Well, sir, I just thought that I could work with Rick...or Sofia," Alex explained.

"Rick is working with Rosa and Sofia with Jacob. You and Liam are a team," Mr. Timothy told him, ending the discussion.

Liam was mortified. First, Alex's lunatic friend had tried to kill him, and now the arrogant jock was embarrassing him in front of the class by refusing to work with him. It was just a goddamned presentation. They were not expected to be best friends for the rest of their lives. *Why is he such a drama queen?*

To Liam's great relief, Alex finally sat next to him. "I'm sorry for the...scene. Of course, I'll work with you," Alex said with some regret in his voice. "That is...assuming you still want to work with me," he added quickly.

Liam was both surprised and confused. He blushed slightly at the attention he was getting from Alex. "Sure," he said shyly.

Both boys were silent for a long time while they were reading the handouts Mr. Timothy had given them. Liam was writing notes in the margins and using marker pens of different colors to highlight the key points. When he reached the last page, he sneaked a glance at Alex. The jock was still on the third page. Liam moved his gaze from Alex's hair to his slim and muscular body. *This project will be so great*, he thought with a smile.

After a moment, Liam looked at Alex again. The boy looked so cute as he focused on the handout. Of course, he always looked cute. And what was great too, after Sam was arrested, Alex and Rick had stopped causing him any trouble at school.

Unfortunately, Alex hadn't paid much attention to him at all. If anything, he was polite but distant. Liam hoped this pair work would let him get to know Alex a bit better and maybe even become friends with him.

Finally, the bell rang. Liam was about to ask Alex when they would continue working on the presentation, but Sofia appeared and literally pushed Alex out of the classroom. Liam couldn't help checking out Alex's butt, which was perfect as always. What was not perfect was Sofia's hand on it.

Liam met Jacob in the corridor, and the boys walked together toward the chemistry classroom. Jacob talked about ice hockey, which didn't surprise Liam, but he listened politely.

"You don't mind working on the history project with Alex's girlfriend?" Liam asked.

"Not at all. She's super-hot! And besides, you're working with Sofia's boyfriend," Jacob replied before he understood what he had just said. "Well, I didn't mean that you and Alex are…I mean…. Well, just forget what I said."

As Jacob tried to explain his logic, Liam was blushing. Had Alex been a girl, Liam could have told Jacob that he had a crush on Alex. Now, he had to hide his feelings while listening as Jacob moved on to a very detailed description of Sofia's boobs and butt. Life wasn't always fair.

Liam was worried about his new friend's reaction if he told Jacob that he fancied Alex's muscular chest and tight butt more than Sofia's female versions. So he just smiled and agreed that Sofia was gorgeous, though the put-on made him want to vomit mentally.

The school day continued with no big surprises, and before Liam realized it, he was packing his books to go home. He hadn't found an opportunity to discuss the history presentation with Alex, and since Alex would already be on his way to swim practice, Liam decided to talk with him the next day. He didn't want to do the work alone.

"How was your school day, dear?" Liam's mother asked as he closed the front door and removed his winter jacket. Though Liam had no siblings, the rack in the hallway was always full of clothes.

"It was great," he replied as his mother straightened her suit and sprayed far too much perfume on her neck.

"I have the evening shift, and I need to go now. You father will be here in an hour. Will you be okay?" his mother asked, sounding worried.

"I'm a big boy. I guess I can manage for an hour without you or Dad," Liam answered and rolled his eyes.

The accident at the beginning of December clearly bothered his mother. She wasn't over it, and neither was he. If Alex hadn't pulled the steering wheel, Liam would have been dead. He hadn't seen the truck coming until the very last moment. When he jumped, he hit his head on something and had lost consciousness for a while. Fortunately, the doctor had said that there was no permanent damage.

Unfortunately, Patrick hadn't been so lucky. Like Liam, he had been one of the kids walking to the Christmas market. As Sam's truck slid uncontrollably on the icy street, it hit Patrick. The swimmer was already dead when the ambulance arrived.

Liam and his mother had visited Patrick's grave on Christmas Day. In some weird way, Liam felt that fate had switched their roles. It should have been Liam who was sleeping in that grave. At least, that had been Sam's plan.

Liam's thoughts switched back to Alex. He had been thinking about Alex a lot lately. There was no question that Alex was the most handsome guy in the school and that Liam had fallen for him. On the other hand, it bothered Liam that Alex had been part of the gas station robbery and the accident.

Alex was dating Sofia, but Liam was still happy Mr. Timothy had paired them for the history presentation. Maybe that was fate as well, and with some luck, he might make a new friend, a very handsome one. The very next moment, Liam felt shallow being so obsessed with Alex's good looks and worried that Alex was just an empty shell without a pearl inside.

"Should I tell my parents I'm gay?" Liam asked his reflection in the mirror. It didn't answer and looked as confused as he was.

Keeping such a big secret from his parents was eating at him. He was close to them, and he was worried that coming out to them would change things. *Will they see me differently? What if they're not proud of me anymore?*

After the accident, Liam had delayed his plan to come out. He didn't want to shock his parents more. The fact that their son had almost died had upset them enough. Now things were gradually getting back to normal, but he never felt the moment was right to deliver the message. And even if it had been, he wouldn't have been able to find the right words.

The opening of the front door interrupted his contemplation. Soon, his father's face appeared in his bedroom door. "Do you want some pizza?" he asked. "I bought some on my way home. I didn't have time for a proper meal at work."

Liam smiled and followed him to the kitchen. They ate their pizza and wondered what Mom would think about their healthy dinner. Together, they agreed not to say a word.

"Sorry about yesterday. I thought you wouldn't want to work with me because of the accident," Alex said when he sat down next to Liam, who seemed tongue-tied. It was five past eleven, and history class had just started.

"It's okay. We can forget that," Liam said finally.

"Cool," Alex replied, not knowing what else to say.

Alex listened carefully as Liam explained the notes and observations he had made from Mr. Timothy's handouts. He was amazed at how much information Liam had gathered. The handouts had been full of difficult terms and confusing details, and he was happy he had been paired with such a genius.

Next, they discussed how they would structure the presentation and what additional information they needed. Alex found it funny that Liam asked for his approval for every decision, despite clearly knowing how the presentation should be done. Alex had hardly anything to add, so he simply agreed with Liam's proposals since the boy certainly needed some encouragement.

When the class ended, Alex was surprised by how much they had accomplished. He packed his things quickly but stayed and waited for Liam, who was more meticulous in putting his belongings into his bag.

"Let's take our bags to our lockers and go get some lunch," Alex said. Liam followed him out of the classroom.

The cafeteria was serving grilled chicken, mashed potatoes, and grated carrots. Alex shoveled his plate full of food and looked for an empty table. Soon, they found one and sat down.

"I'm starving! Luckily, this is edible," Alex said after swallowing a bite.

"Yeah, and it's nicer to eat at the table than on the floor," Liam said.

"I'm so sorry. Sam was an idiot sometimes," Alex replied, feeling embarrassed.

"It's not your fault," Liam said quickly and blushed slightly.

Soon Rick, Rosa, and Sofia arrived and joined them. Sofia sat next to Alex and glared at Liam.

"How's your project going with Jacob?" Alex asked Sofia.

"It's okay," Sofia said shortly.

"How's the gay couple doing?" Rick joked, referring to Alex and Liam. All the other boys had been paired with girls. Alex and Liam were working together because there were more boys than girls in the class.

"Our work is going well," Liam answered quickly before Alex could swallow all the food that was in his mouth.

"We're going to Rick's house to work on our project tonight," Rosa said.

She glanced at Rick, who had a goofy smile on his face. "Indeed," he said finally, and his smile seemed to get wider.

"Would you like to come to my place tonight? We have some more work to do, too," Alex asked. It took Liam a moment to realize Alex was talking to him.

"Huh? Sure. That's fine," he replied.

"Good, it's agreed, then," Alex said casually. He continued eating, totally oblivious to Sofia's acid glare.

"You are so lucky. Liam's such a genius," Rosa said to Alex. She smiled at Liam.

"Miss 'music is my whole life' Pearson is making us write an essay about some boring movie that she showed us in music class," she continued. "Liam finished it in, like, ten minutes."

"Great. Then I'm in good hands," Alex said enthusiastically. He didn't notice that Rick tried to muffle a laugh or that Sofia continued to glare at him silently for the rest of lunch.

When the school day ended at three o'clock, Alex walked to the swimming hall with Rick. They had a two-hour practice that day, and he had agreed to meet

Liam after that. He thought they could do homework together and then continue to work on their history presentation.

The boys took quick showers, dressed in their speedos, and walked to the pool.

"I'm still not used to Sam and Patrick not being here," Rick said with sadness in his voice.

"Me neither," Alex replied. Even though Sam had been his friend, Alex couldn't help feeling he had gotten what he deserved. Did that make Alex a lousy friend?

What Alex missed were all those discussions with Patrick. While the other boys were more interested in girls and swimming, Patrick was the only one he could talk to about his plans for the future. Alex felt he was growing apart from his childhood friends and that he had just lost the one he would have wanted to keep. It was scary and sad.

"Okay, guys," Coach Hanson said, choosing his words carefully, "we've gone through some difficult times. Two of us are not here anymore, but the rest of us need to keep going."

After Patrick's death and Sam's arrest, the joint decision had been made to stop practices for a while. The team had met a couple of times a week at the swimming hall, and they had mostly spent those times just hanging out together in the pool. Nobody felt any real desire to practice, but they appreciated each other's company.

Coach Hanson asked the team if they felt ready to continue training. Everybody nodded, and they began with a warm-up. Alex did push-ups and sit-ups on the floor, then he jumped into the water and swam to the other side of the pool as fast as he could. It felt great for his body and mind. He hadn't felt this happy and energetic for weeks.

"What do you think about Liam?" Rick asked him when they were taking showers after practice.

"What do you mean?" Alex replied.

"Well, there are some rumors."

"What rumors?"

"Um…Sam said he's…gay," Rick said quietly.

"And you believe everything that Sam said? He killed our friend!" Alex shouted, staring at Rick.

"Sorry, forget I mentioned Sam," Rick said quickly. "I just suspect that Liam isn't playing on the same team as us."

"I don't know where he plays, and besides, it's not like we're friends or something. We were just asked to prepare a presentation together," Alex said and realized that he sounded like he was making excuses for something.

The way Rick kept looking at him made Alex feel uncomfortable. "And do I really need to remind you that I'm dating Sofia?" he said and realized that Rick had just forced him to cancel his plan to focus on school instead of girls.

Feeling irritated, Rick changed the subject, and they finished their showers. As they drove home in Alex's car, they hardly spoke. What Rick had said about Liam bothered Alex, but he decided to ignore Rick's comments. He stopped in front of Rick's house, let his friend out of the car, and drove home.

He thought about Liam. He and his friends had bullied the poor boy for the whole semester, and after all that, Liam still wanted to come to his house and work on a project with him. Alex felt ashamed of his behavior. *The boy must have a big heart.*

Chapter 8

Liam closed his front door and hurried toward Alex's house, wanting to run in his excitement. He couldn't believe he would soon meet the blond swimmer and spend some time with him in his home. They were hardly friends, but this was so much more than he could have dreamed of when he first met the jock in September.

Finally, Liam had arrived. He admired the big house. Alex's parents must be wealthy. In a house like that, one could easily have raised an entire tribe, but he remembered hearing Alex was their only child. After walking through the front yard, Liam pressed the doorbell and heard the chime, then some footsteps.

"Um…good evening, sir. Is Alex home?" he finally said, just as Alex's father opened his mouth to ask what he wanted.

"Sure, come in. I'm Mr. Wesley, Alex's father, as you might have guessed already."

Alex ran down the stairs to welcome Liam. He was handsome, as always. Liam realized he was staring at Alex and quickly turned to hang his winter coat on the rack and to take his shoes off. Then the boys went upstairs to Alex's room.

The room was big and bright with light gray walls and hardwood floor, which felt warm under Liam's feet. It was in the corner of the house, and there were windows on two walls. The long curtains fit the stylish decoration perfectly and Alex's mother had, most likely, selected the paintings. Alex's towel and speedo were hanging on the back of a seat.

"Sorry, it's a bit of a mess in here. If you don't mind, we can sit on my bed," Alex said and pointed to the big bed on the other side of the room.

First time at his house, and we are already in his bed, Liam thought but decided not to say it aloud. Luckily, Alex didn't notice the grin on his face. The boys took comfortable positions on the red bedspread and started to do their homework.

After Liam had finished his homework and helped Alex finish his, they began to work on the history presentation. They spread the handouts on the bed, and Liam took notes with his laptop while Alex did his best to find the relevant information on the papers.

Liam realized that, every now and then, Alex glanced at him when he didn't think Liam would notice. This made Liam uncomfortable—he assumed Alex was still assessing him, and he worried that Alex might not like him very much. He tried to focus on the presentation and on not making a fool of himself, carefully considering all his words and avoiding saying anything that Alex might find stupid or funny in the wrong way.

The tactic worked. Alex behaved properly toward him—he was even nice to him. Liam was feeling optimistic that they could finish the presentation without any serious friction.

For the first time since entering Alex's house, Liam started to relax a little. Noticing he had been sweating and his armpits were wet, he felt embarrassed and changed his position to hide this from Alex.

They had worked on the presentation for over an hour when Alex surprised him with a question. "Would you like to play some games?" Alex asked as he switched on his PlayStation.

Liam was delighted. Either the blond swimmer really enjoyed spending time with him, or he was just tired of doing schoolwork. Either way, Liam was more than eager to play some games, and they spent the next two hours doing so.

"Dude, you really can play *Call of Duty*," Alex said with admiration in his voice. Liam had beaten him quite a few times, and Alex clearly hadn't expected that to happen.

"Well, it's not exactly the first time I've played this," Liam said modestly, grinning at Alex. "Gosh, I didn't realize it was so late already," he said, checking his watch. It was past nine. "I better go home before your parents kick me out," he said half-jokingly.

"I don't think they will, but do you want to come back over tomorrow to work on our history project?" Alex asked.

"Sure," Liam answered, worried that he sounded too eager.

Liam couldn't keep the goofy smile off his face while he walked home. It was probably anatomically impossible for a human being to form a wider smile than he had. Alex wasn't only stunningly gorgeous, but he seemed to be a cool guy, too. And, most importantly, he wanted to see Liam again.

Alex is just a friend, Liam reminded himself. Actually, being friends with Alex was all that Liam wanted. He wasn't crazy enough to fantasize about Alex as his boyfriend. Besides, jocks fell in love with nerds only in teenage novels and TV shows. Liam understood such things hardly ever happened in real life, but that didn't spoil his good mood.

Liam had felt lonely ever since Matthew disappeared from his life over eighteen months ago. For months after Matthew's family had moved away, Liam had waited for his friend to visit or at least to contact him somehow. He had spent many nights sitting on his bed, waiting for a call that never came. But tonight, Alex began to fill a part of the gap that Matthew had left in Liam's heart. Well, that was until he got home.

"What did you just say? You were where?" His mother's voice was so loud that half the neighborhood must have heard her question. Liam's father rushed into the kitchen to see why his wife was so upset.

"I was at Alex's house. We worked on our history presentation and played some video games," Liam explained as calmly as he could.

"But that's the same boy whose friend almost killed you!" his mother yelled. "I really don't like you spending time with that boy."

"But the teacher asked us to work together," Liam explained, not feeling so calm anymore.

"I'll call the principal tomorrow morning. They need to assign you a new partner," she said determinedly.

"No! You won't call anybody. Besides, Alex is a nice guy, and I…" Liam trailed off, not knowing how to complete the sentence. He would never forgive his mother if she ruined his emerging friendship with Alex. In his dismay, he had almost let it slip that he had a crush on the boy.

They sat down to talk, and Liam explained their history assignment and what they had done at Alex's house. He described Alex to his parents on a general level, keeping his special interest in him well hidden. Liam wanted to tell his parents he was gay, but this wasn't the right moment. His only goal was to convince his parents that he could see Alex again.

Finally, Liam's mother agreed that the boys could continue working on the history presentation.

"If he ever tries to do anything to you, he'll answer to me," she said firmly.

Liam was able to breathe again. He wished his parents a good night and went to his room. After turning on his laptop, Liam re-read the paper he had written with Alex for the history presentation.

He emailed the document to Alex and would have included a personal message if he had only been able to find the right words. What would straight boys write to each other? He had just pressed the send button when he saw his mother at his door.

"Liam, I'm sorry about our fight," she said as she sat on his bed. "Of course, I want you to find friends at school." She smiled at him.

"Alex is really a cool guy," Liam said.

She nodded. "I trust you. Are you hungry? Would you like to eat something before you go to bed?"

Actually, Liam was starving. He put away a big piece of blueberry pie with some milk and figured his mother was trying to make up for their argument with the treat. He dreamed that, someday, he could introduce Alex to his parents as his boyfriend and they could all eat blueberry pie together in their kitchen. But it was wishful thinking, and he knew it.

After the sweet and tasty supper, Liam went to bed but couldn't sleep. He was thinking of Alex and the time they had spent in his house. The jock had been wearing a tight shirt that outlined his lean body. Liam felt his groin stirring when a picture of Alex's cute butt filled his mind. Half an hour later, he fell asleep with a broad smile on his face.

The alarm clock went off, and Alex woke up, turning on his computer. He read the the document from Liam and admired how fluent and insightful Liam's writing was. He could have never written such a smart summary from such complex details.

They had agreed to continue their work today, intending to dig into Finland's role in the events that led to the Paris Peace Treaties. Alex couldn't understand how the small northern country had been able to defend itself against the massive forces of the Soviet Union. He was sure Liam could explain it to him.

"How are you doing with your history presentation?" Alex's mother asked as he stood in the kitchen, filling his bowl with cereal.

"Very well," Alex said. "Well, it's mostly because of Liam," he admitted.

His mother put the newspaper on the table and looked at her son. "It's good you've found such a smart friend," she said.

Alex expected another fight about what bad company his swimming team friends were, but his mother just wished him a good day at school and told him about an important meeting she would have with a big client. After she left for work, Alex finished his breakfast quickly and took a shower.

He had hardly stepped out of his car in the school's parking lot when Sofia rushed up to talk to him.

"Hi, Alex! Do you have any plans for this evening?" she asked.

Alex checked his watch—there were still fifteen minutes before the first class started. He would have to answer Sofia's question, which was clearly supposed to lead to their getting together after school. Waiting for the answer, Sofia took hold of his hand, and they walked toward the school.

"Um…unfortunately, I have swim practice today," Alex said.

Sofia tried again. "Can I come to your house after practice?"

"Sorry, but I already agreed to meet Liam," Alex said, avoiding Sofia's gaze. They walked for a moment in silence.

"You spent the whole day with Liam yesterday, too," Sofia said sadly. "If you don't like me, just say it," she continued with an accusing tone.

"Of course I like you!" Alex said quickly. "I just don't have time today."

Sofia didn't say anything but stormed on her way as soon as she had put her books in her locker. Alex sighed and headed toward his class, hoping she would calm down sooner or later. Probably later.

After a couple of classes, it was lunchtime. Alex filled his plate with sausage soup and took a seat at an empty table. Rick followed him, sat down, and looked around to make sure nobody could hear him.

"So, you dumped Sofia and turned into a fairy," he said bluntly.

"What?" Alex shouted, stunned.

"Rosa told me you and Sofia are no longer together, and you are hanging out with Liam," Rick said. His voice was more questioning than blaming.

"Goddamn Sofia! What the fuck is wrong with her?" Alex cursed. "I told her I don't have time today because we have swim practice, and then I need to work on the history presentation. Why do chicks need to be such drama queens?"

Rick smiled. "Clearly, you don't know how to handle your girl," he mocked. "Dude, listen. Whatever she says, just agree with it. You'll be rewarded," he said with a smirk.

"I see," Alex said, even though he wasn't too convinced.

Soon, Liam arrived with his tray and looked at Alex, asking silently if it was okay to sit at his table. Alex looked uncomfortable but smiled at Liam and nodded toward the empty seat next to him. Liam sat down, looking grateful. The three boys ate in total silence, and Alex noticed Rick was constantly glancing at Liam.

"If we're able to finish the next part of the history presentation, I'll kick your ass in *Call of Duty* again," Liam said to break the silence. Alex raised his head and saw Rick's surprised expression.

"So, you weren't working on your presentation yesterday," Rick observed.

"Sure we were. But do you seriously think that I could work on some boring presentation the whole night?" Alex said.

Rick sipped some milk from his glass. "Have you played a lot?" he asked Liam.

They talked about video games for the rest of lunch. Alex was mostly silent, following the discussion between Liam and Rick. Sofia and Rosa were sitting at their own table watching the boys. Alex tried to smile at Sofia, but she turned her head away.

In math class, Sofia made it clear to Alex that he wasn't welcome to sit with her. He snorted with laughter at the childish girl and took an empty seat next to Liam.

"Great. I could use some advice from a math genius," Liam said, delighted. The teacher left to fetch some handouts he had forgotten, and while he was gone, Alex explained the solution to their last homework assignment to Liam. Sofia glared at them from the back of the room.

The school day continued normally, and the only exception to the routine was Sofia, who was in one of her moods. Alex tried to keep out of her way, annoyed by her short temper. By the last class, she seemed to be in a better mood again, and Alex could take his typical seat next to her. The atmosphere between them wasn't really warm, but at least she was talking to him again.

When the class ended, Alex said goodbye to Sofia and headed to the swimming hall. Sofia was still downbeat, but she wished Alex a good practice. He was hopeful he could fix his relationship with her despite the girl being anything but easy to get along with.

"Have you gotten past first base with Sofia?" Rick asked him in the shower after practice.

"Or second base?" Eric joked. His parents were from Colombia, but he had lived his whole life in Fairmont and was the same age as Rick and Alex.

Alex smirked at his teammates. "All in good time," he said, not feeling comfortable giving a detailed explanation of what he had done, or in this case hadn't done, with Sofia. Compared to what he had heard other boys talk about doing with their girlfriends, he didn't have much to brag about, but he still wanted to take things slowly with Sofia.

"Don't be too slow, or someone will take her from you," Eric advised him.

"Nobody's going to take my girl anywhere," Alex said, acting offended.

"Then you need to act like a man. Girls like real men," Eric teased, showing off his muscles.

"I'll show you who's a real man," Alex shouted, playing along. He threw his wet speedo at Eric. The suit hit Eric in the stomach, which was close but not exactly what he had aimed for. Eric picked up the speedo from the floor and threw it over the wall into the pool area.

"Thanks dude. How am I going to get it back?" Alex asked, pointing at his naked body.

"Just go over there. It's so small that nobody can see it," Eric joked, but he put on his speedo and got Alex's swimming trunks for him.

After the other boys had left the showers, Rick said to Alex, "You need to talk with Sofia. I mean, really talk. She was clearly avoiding you all day."

"No shit, Sherlock," Alex said. "Okay, okay. Maybe I could ask her to come to the mall with me tomorrow. I need new jeans anyway."

"Sounds like a plan," Rick said.

They left the swimming hall, and Alex drove home. He was happy Rick had stopped pressing him about Liam and they had actually gotten along pretty well during lunch. He didn't need any more drama in his life. Patrick had died, Sam was in prison, and Sofia's mood was constantly shifting from one extreme to the other.

Right now, all he wanted was to finish the presentation and play some video games.

Alex was already waiting in the hallway when Liam pressed the doorbell. "Hi, come in," Alex said, and Liam followed the instruction happily. They went upstairs to Alex's room.

"How was practice?" Liam asked when he saw Alex's swimming equipment drying.

"It was great. I set a new record," Alex said enthusiastically. He explained to Liam what they typically did during practice.

Liam had to admit he was more interested in seeing Alex in his speedo than in the details of the swimming team practice, but he listened attentively. When Alex finished, they sat on his bed and began to work on their history presentation.

"How do you think we should present this to the class?" Alex asked after they had worked intensively for almost two hours.

"I was thinking we could split the presentation into four parts and present them in turns. If you don't mind, I can start," Liam proposed.

"That's cool," Alex said. He smiled, realizing Liam had everything under perfect control.

"Can I borrow your laptop? I want to check something," Alex asked, reaching for Liam's laptop.

"Sure," Liam said and gave it to Alex, who opened the browser and started typing.

"What the fuck!" Alex shouted. "Your Google search history is full of some gay stuff." He looked at Liam, who blushed quickly.

Liam was thinking rapidly. What could he say? He wasn't ashamed of being gay, but he was worried about Alex's reaction. Also, he didn't want the whole school to know. High school was difficult enough for a kid who had just moved from another city, and he had finally started to make friends.

"Are you…?" Alex asked. He was standing in the middle of his room. He couldn't even finish the question, but Liam was well aware of what he meant. Finally, Liam raised his face and looked Alex in the eyes.

"Yes, I am," he said so quietly that Alex barely heard him. There was no point in lying. His browsing history was undeniable evidence.

He looked at Alex, scared, and his heart was pounding. Alex walked to the window and looked out. For a long moment, he didn't say anything. Finally, he turned around.

"I guess it's okay," he said, but Liam wasn't sure if he really meant it.

"It's not contagious," Liam tried to joke, and Alex let out a forced laugh.

They worked on the presentation for another half hour, but Liam could feel the atmosphere had changed. Once they were finished, he stored the results of their work on his laptop, but as he walked home, he realized they hadn't agreed on their next meeting time. There had been no *Call of Duty* tournament this evening, either. Apparently, their friendship was over before it had really started.

The only good thing that had happened was Alex had promised not to tell anybody at school. Liam hoped he could trust Alex on this. When he got home, he went straight to his bed and cried until he fell asleep.

Chapter 9

Alex saw Rick in the school parking lot the following morning. Rick had been right about Liam. Liam was gay. Alex had assumed it was just a stupid rumor Sam had spread to torment Liam.

But maybe that's what it was, Alex reasoned. It was unlikely that Liam had come out to Sam and Rick, which meant they must have made a lucky guess. Regardless, Alex decided not to confirm it to Rick. He had promised Liam that he would keep his secret, and he didn't want anybody to know he had been playing video games in his house with a gay guy.

"Did Liam beat your ass in *Call of Duty* again?" Rick asked as they left the parking lot.

"No. We were just working on the presentation," Alex replied. He didn't want it to sound that he and

Liam were more than two students who were asked to work together.

"Since we don't have practice today, I'm taking Sofia to the mall to buy some new clothes," Alex said. He wanted to take the conversation in another direction: his girlfriend.

I don't have anything to hide. I'm dating Sofia, and Liam is the one who is gay, Alex calmed himself.

Rick looked at him and asked, "You mean you've sorted out all your arguments?"

"I called Sofia this morning and asked her to meet up after school. That was all it took to make her happy again." Alex smiled.

They started talking about Rick and Rosa's latest date, and Alex felt everything was again as it should be. Maybe they could even agree on a double date some weekend.

Alex sat with Sofia during history class. The presentations were to begin that period so he couldn't have worked with Liam anyway. He didn't want to give the impression that he and Liam were friends, but his heart bled a little when he saw how sad Liam looked sitting alone on the other side of the classroom.

Alex didn't want to hurt Liam. The boy was kind and friendly. He just had an impossible choice in front of him. When the class ended, Alex left the classroom with Sofia, avoiding eye contact with Liam.

Lunch break didn't make life any easier for Alex. He chose an empty table and was delighted that Liam understood not to sit with him. Still, he couldn't help glancing at Liam during lunch, and every time he saw the sad boy eating his hamburger alone, he felt like a traitor.

Soon, Sofia, Rick, and Rosa came with their trays. Sofia, beaming, sat next to Alex, and Rick took a seat on the opposite side of the table. Rosa was about to sit next to her boyfriend when she saw Liam at the other table.

"Honey, is it okay if I sit with Liam?" she asked and left before Rick could say anything. Alex and Rick looked at each other. Sofia barely noticed that Rosa had left; she had everything she wanted. She had Alex.

The school day continued, and just before English class, Alex finally got a chance to talk alone with Rick.

"Why did Rosa want to eat with Liam?" he asked, going straight to the topic.

"I don't know. I tried to ask, but she just said they had some private things they wanted to talk about." There was irritation in Rick's voice. "I don't like my girlfriend hanging around with that fag."

"Dude, don't say that to Rosa," Alex said "You know what a Good Samaritan she is."

"No kidding. And don't worry. I'm not an idiot," Rick snorted.

When the last class ended, Alex drove to the mall with Sofia. They went to a small store that sold mostly men's clothes. Alex bought most of his clothes there because the staff was friendly and they had an unbelievable knack for finding jeans and shirts that Alex liked. Sofia held Alex's hand, smiling like the Cheshire cat.

"How can I help you?" the salesclerk asked politely, giving the young couple a smile. She was in her forties and dressed in a nice suit that fit her age. She wore a nametag that read, "Jenny Green."

"Well, I need new jeans," Alex said.

"Actually, the new collection from Diesel just arrived," she said and scanned Alex from head to toe. Then she picked a couple of jeans from the shelf.

"This red design has been quite popular and would fit well on such a handsome young man," she said. Alex blushed slightly.

"We have blue and black ones, too," the salesclerk said when she noticed some hesitation on his part. Alex decided to give the red ones a chance and marched into the fitting room with the jeans and a black-and-white shirt.

"The young man clearly has good taste," the clerk said when Alex opened the fitting room door. With that, it was a done deal.

"You could've asked my opinion, too," Sofia said disappointedly when they sat down to wait for their food in a fast food restaurant. Alex had ordered a hamburger while Sofia asked for water and their lowest-calorie salad.

"Um…sorry. These looked so cool that I knew immediately I wanted them," Alex said, pointing to the bag containing his new clothes. "Don't you like them?" he asked cautiously. He couldn't understand why he needed Sofia's approval to buy some clothes, but he didn't want to upset her either.

"They are nice," Sofia said shortly and looked out the window.

While waiting for their food, Alex looked at the boy behind the counter. He was a high school student, most likely a senior. *Patrick worked part-time in this restaurant, too*, Alex thought, realizing this was the first time he had eaten here since Patrick's death.

Alex suddenly missed his friend enormously. He decided not to share his feelings with Sofia, who was now complaining that the restaurant was dirty and the staff slow and unfriendly.

After they had finished their meal, Alex asked Sofia if she wanted to go home. She insisted on spending some more time with him. They soon found their way to Alex's house, which was empty since his parents had gone to a movie.

Alex took a couple of soft drinks from the fridge, and they went to his room. He gave a drink to Sofia and sat in a chair. For a long time, he couldn't think of anything to say. Sofia also sat quietly on his bed and looked at him.

"Would you like to play something?" Alex asked finally and offered Sofia a video game controller. She didn't take it.

"Could we just talk or something?" she replied.

"Okay. Well, what do you want to talk about?" Alex asked, putting the controller away.

"You need to kiss me first," Sofia said seductively.

Alex rose from his chair and sat on the bed. Their lips moved closer and closer until he felt Sofia's smooth and moist lips. Far too soon, Alex pulled his head back and opened his eyes.

"Only one?" Sofia asked, moving her body closer to Alex. He felt her hands on his thighs, climbing toward his crotch.

"Wait," Alex said. "My parents might come home soon." He moved away from Sofia.

"Maybe I should go then," Sofia said before she got up and walked downstairs.

Alex followed. "See you tomorrow at school," he said and tried to smile.

"Whatever," Sofia said and slammed the door.

Alex sighed. Apparently, Sofia was mad at him again. He wondered if he should call her and apologize, but he wasn't entirely sure what to apologize for. He was tired of Sofia's temper. *She's probably the hottest chick in school. How on earth will I explain it to the guys if I break up with her?*

Or maybe it was just that he didn't know how to date. Girls should be equipped with a user's manual. At least, Sofia's constantly changing mood was beyond his understanding.

Alex walked back to his room and picked up the video game controller. He would have called Rick and asked him to come over, but that wasn't an option since Rick had a date with Rosa. For a moment, Alex considered calling Liam, but he couldn't find the courage to grab his phone.

Liam had spent the weekend at a music camp that Fairmont's music department had organized in a cozy old log house in the mountains near the city of St.

Richards. It was more than one hundred and fifty miles from Fairmont, but his father had offered to drive him there. Liam had played the piano since he was seven years old, and over the years, he had become pretty good at it.

"Your performance was really great. I am so proud of you," Liam's father said in the car on their way home. The students had played in a concert, where the parents had been invited to watch.

"Yeah, it was pretty okay," Liam replied.

They drove the first fifty miles in total silence. Now that the camp had ended, Liam felt sad again. Alex had avoided him ever since he discovered Liam was gay, more than two weeks ago now. However, Alex had kept his promise—he didn't tell the entire school about it. Actually, he was neither hostile nor unfriendly toward Liam, just distant and nonchalant. He avoided any contact between them.

The situation with Alex reminded Liam about a time when he had a major disagreement with Matthew. They had been little kids, less than ten years old, and the reason for the fight had been so childish that Liam was too embarrassed to think of it. Matthew hadn't talked to him for a week, which was a lifetime for kids at that age. Finally, they had patched things up and had become best friends again. Liam hoped it would work as easily with Alex.

Another thing that was bothering him was hiding his feelings from his parents. He was as desperate to come out to them as he was afraid of their reaction. *If being gay is normal, why is it so difficult to talk about it?*

"Penny for your thoughts," his father said, interrupting the silence.

"Um…nothing special. I'm just tired after camp," Liam lied and wondered whether his father would still be proud of him if he knew Liam wanted to date other boys, especially one blond swimmer.

On Monday morning, Liam took his familiar seat in history class. It would soon be his turn to give the presentation with Alex, and Liam was becoming rather worried because they hadn't finished it yet. Actually, they hadn't worked on it at all since the evening that had changed everything.

A large portion of his worry went away when Alex entered the classroom and unexpectedly sat next to him. Alex looked amazingly cute in his new red jeans and black-and-white shirt. Liam couldn't help staring at him.

"I'm sorry. I've been an idiot lately," Alex said and seemed sincere. Despite Alex's handsome looks, Liam was still mad at him and stayed silent.

Alex sighed. "Could we still finish this presentation together? And…I would like to talk with you after class," he said. Liam nodded.

When the class ended, Sofia hurried out of the room without paying any attention to Alex. Liam was surprised for a moment that she didn't stop to talk with her boyfriend, but then realized the couple had probably had yet another quarrel. The on–off characteristic of their relationship hadn't gone unnoticed by anyone at Fairmont High. Some people assumed Alex was lousy boyfriend material, but the majority thought Sofia was just a difficult person.

Liam, Alex, Rick, and Rosa walked from history class to their lockers. "I'll go and ask Sofia if everything is okay," Rosa said, walking after her best friend.

"Um…Rick, I need to talk to Liam…alone," Alex said to Rick, looking uncomfortable. Rick seemed surprised and was about to say something, but then he just nodded and walked toward his next class.

As soon as they were alone, Liam said bluntly, "So, you wanted to talk to me."

"I want to apologize," Alex said. It was awkward, but he tried to look Liam directly in his eyes. "Your…your thing…it kind of surprised me," he said, trying to find the correct words.

Liam's eyes narrowed. "My *thing*? What's my thing?" he asked knowing very well what he meant. The small devil inside him just didn't want to make this too easy for Alex.

"Well…the gay thing, you know," Alex said. He had lost eye contact with Liam, and he was now nervously twisting his fingers.

"Is my gay thing a problem for you?" Liam asked and sounded angry.

"No," Alex said quickly and looked into Liam's eyes again. "That's what I'm trying to say," he said finally. He smiled tentatively at Liam, who calmed down rapidly.

"I want to keep working on the presentation with you," Alex said and waited until Liam nodded. "And…I would like to be friends with you again," he said shyly.

Liam was surprised, but a weak smile appeared on his face.

"Besides, I also need somebody whose ass I can kick in *Call of Duty*," Alex said when he perceived that Liam wasn't angry anymore.

"Well, I can be your friend, but it will be your sorry ass that gets kicked," Liam said as seriously as he could.

"So, we are okay?" Alex asked.

"Yes, but only if you hug me for compensation," Liam said, enjoying the confused look at Alex's face. "Just kidding," he said finally, and Alex laughed nervously.

"Maybe some other time," Alex said and winked. Now it was Liam's turn to be confused.

Liam was happy they were friends again, and for the rest of the day, no matter how hard he tried, he couldn't get rid of the goofy smile on his face. Every time he thought of Alex, his smile got wider and wider. In chemistry class, even Jacob noticed it and asked him why the sun was shining so warmly.

When that class ended and Liam had packed all his books, he left the room to find Alex waiting for him. They walked together to the cafeteria for lunch. The only way Liam could have felt happier was if Alex had held his hand, but he knew that was off limits. They were just friends, and that was more than Liam could have ever hoped for.

"You are taking turns now," Rick said in a loud voice when he sat down at their table. Both boys looked confused.

"Last week you were eating with Sofia. Now it seems to be Liam's turn again," Rick said. "Was the seating order the topic of your secret meeting this morning?"

Liam noticed Alex blushing but neither of them got a chance to answer before Rosa and Sofia arrived. Rosa immediately sat next to Rick, but Sofia chose the seat that was farthest from Alex. Apparently, the girls hadn't yet decided whether to sit with the boys, and Sofia didn't agree with Rosa's choice. Rosa was too focused on Rick to notice her mistake.

"Does it bother you that Rick is joking like we're an item?" Liam asked Alex after they left the dining hall.

"No. And we are not an item," Alex said. "I mean…there's nothing wrong with you…. We could be if I was…you know," he tried to explain.

"I get the point," Liam interrupted him. "And it's good to know there's nothing wrong with me."

"So, no kissing or groping," Alex said and poked Liam's arm in a friendly way.

After Alex's swimming practice, the boys continued working on their history presentation at Alex's house. They finished it in less than two hours, and Alex asked Liam if he would like to go skating on the river. He was surprised to hear Liam hadn't skated for years. Alex gave him his old skates, and they walked to the river. It was freezing outside, and they agreed to skate for only a short distance.

They skated for some twenty minutes and enjoyed the beautiful scenery. Then Liam wanted to turn back since his toes and fingers had begun to feel like icicles. Alex pushed Liam from behind to give him some more speed, and in fifteen minutes, they were back where they had started.

"That was fun," Liam said, smiling. Fifty yards ahead was the familiar shore where they had left their shoes. Despite the freezing weather, he stopped to look at the houses on the riverbank.

"Let's get you in before you turn into an ice sculpture," Alex said.

"Let me try this again," Liam said, and he started to skate backward. Alex had shown him how to do that.

Liam's efforts looked clumsy, and he had trouble staying up. He kept skating, persistently moving toward the shore with his back leading the way. Every now and then, he strayed from the plowed route, which wasn't a big problem since there wasn't much snow on the ice.

"LOOK OUT!" Alex shouted suddenly.

There was a hole in the ice that some people had made to try winter swimming. There were warning signs around the hole, but Liam couldn't see them when skating backward and had wandered off the plowed route again. Alex watched, terrified, as Liam skated directly into the hole.

Chapter 10

Liam flapped his legs and hands. It took a moment before he could stand up in the icy water. The hole was hardly ten feet wide, and the river was not deep. Still, he was up to his chest in the water. He tried desperately to get up onto the ice, but his wet clothes were heavy and the ice around the hole was slippery. He couldn't get himself out.

"Please, help me!" he yelled to Alex, who had already skated over and kneeled down to help him. With one strong pull, Alex lifted Liam out of the water.

"Thanks," Liam said, shivering.

Alex helped Liam to remove his skates and put on his winter boots. Then the boys hurried to Alex's home. It was already getting dark, and the temperature was decreasing. When they got inside, Alex took Liam directly to the bathroom.

"Let's get your wet clothes off," Alex said and started to undress Liam, who was still shocked and shaking.

When Liam's jacket and shirt were off, Alex hesitated a bit before opening Liam's belt and unbuttoning his jeans. He pulled Liam's jeans down and raised his legs to get them off completely.

"Um…maybe you want to take off your boxers yourself," he said. Liam slowly pulled his boxers down. It was a major embarrassment to stand naked in front of Alex. He saw Alex checking him out and tried to cover his manhood.

"It's because of the cold water," he said, trying to defend his dignity.

Alex laughed. "Okay, hung boy, let's get you under the warm shower," he said and opened the shower curtain.

Liam blushed but stepped under the water. Quickly, he pulled the curtain shut so Alex couldn't see him. His penis was waking up, and he wanted to avoid any further embarrassment.

"There's a towel for you on the bench," Alex said and left to change his clothes. Liam felt relieved when he heard the bathroom door close. The warm water felt good on his body and he wanted to stay there as long as possible. After the shower, Liam wrapped the towel tightly around his waist and walked upstairs to find Alex.

"I got some dry clothes for you. They might be a little big," Alex said, pointing to a pile of clothes.

Stacked nicely on his bed were a set of black socks, white boxers, gray sweatpants, and a white t-shirt.

Liam looked at the clothes. "You don't mind me wearing your clothes?" he asked finally.

"I would mind more if you walked around naked," Alex said and grinned.

Reluctantly, Liam began to dress in front of Alex, using the towel as a cover. His friend was clearly amused when he used his teeth to hold the towel while pulling on Alex's boxers. Luckily, Alex decided to give him some privacy and turned his head away. Ultimately, Liam managed to get dressed.

"Do you feel okay? I mean, do you want me to take you to the hospital or anything?" Alex asked.

"No, thanks. I'm fine," Liam replied.

Alex took hold of Liam's left hand and then his right. "At least your hands feel warm."

"Yeah, I think I will survive."

"Are you hungry?" Alex asked. He walked to the kitchen before Liam could say anything, took a pizza from the freezer, and put it into the oven. While he waited for the pizza to cook, he set the table. Liam watched as Alex was preparing their supper and couldn't help noticing how enthusiastic his friend looked.

"This is delicious!" Liam said when he tasted the pizza, which Alex had pimped with some extra cheese he found in the fridge. Alex smiled at the compliment.

I wish this was a date, Liam thought and felt happy and sad at the same time. It was nice to eat and talk about the skating trip with Alex, but at the same time, he had to remind himself they were just friends.

After their supper, Alex drove Liam home. He didn't walk Liam to the door, which finally broke Liam's illusion of being on a date. Nevertheless, it had been a great evening, especially if he forgot the freezing water and the embarrassing shower episode. The best thing was that Alex had promised to come over to Liam's house the next day, after his swimming practice.

"What has he done to you?" Liam's mother yelled when he walked in and she saw his wet clothes.

"Mom, calm down, and I'll explain everything. This is not Alex's fault," he said. His mother waited for an explanation, but the doorbell interrupted Liam, who ran to answer the door.

"You forgot your bag," Alex said and passed the bag to Liam, whose mother appeared at the door. Alex, who had never met Liam's mother, offered his hand.

"Good evening, Mrs. Green," he said and realized he was shaking hands with the same salesclerk who had sold him his jeans and shirt some weeks ago.

"Hi, Alex. It's nice to finally see you. Liam has been talking about you a lot," Liam's mother said. She seemed to have recognized Alex.

"I hope he has been saying good things about me," Alex said.

"For sure, he has," she replied, emphasizing her words. Liam blushed.

"Well, I should go now," Alex said and left after saying goodbye to Liam and his mother.

Liam explained to his parents what had happened when he and Alex were skating. His mother would have wanted to call Alex and thank him, but Liam managed to convince her that she could thank Alex the next day when he came over.

"He's coming here tomorrow?" Liam's mother asked. "Oh, dear. I need to visit the grocery store after work. Do you think he likes chicken pasta and garlic bread?" She had started her typical fuss.

Liam watched as his mother arranged things in the living room and kitchen. She asked his father to get the vacuum cleaner. While his father was cleaning, she browsed her recipes. Liam was happy his mother had evidently accepted Alex as his friend. The hullabaloo occurring in their house was clear evidence of it.

When the house was neat and clean, Liam went to bed. He was thinking of Alex and how gorgeous he was. "Alex is straight," Liam said to himself. It felt bad, but he had to accept the reality, or he would never get over his obsession. Liam decided that, after high school, he would get a boyfriend. Until then, he would enjoy his friendship with Alex. It felt like the right decision.

The rising sun woke the sleepy boy. An hour later, after falling asleep again for a while, Liam rose from his bed and pushed the curtains aside. It was the last week of March, and the snow had started to disappear from their backyard. Spring was coming.

Two months had passed since Liam had fallen into the hole in the river ice. The boys had become good friends, and they spent a lot of time together doing homework and even more time playing video games.

Liam still took every opportunity to check out Alex's butt or crotch and enjoyed what he saw. But the worst of his obsession was over, and he had accepted that they were just friends. He was sure Alex had noticed his glances, but Alex didn't seem to mind.

Liam checked the time on the clock on his bedside table. It was nine-thirty on Saturday morning. Alex would soon pick him up—they had planned to drive to the big mall in Buonas, roughly fifty miles from Fairmont. Their plan was to spend the morning shopping for new clothes, have lunch in the afternoon, and then see a movie in the big theater that had been built next to the mall a year ago.

All the mirrors in the bathroom were full of steam when Liam finally turned off the water and stepped out of the shower. His parents constantly complained that he wasted hot water, but he loved long showers. After wrapping his towel around his waist, he hurried to his room and almost walked into Alex, who was standing in the room and looking at the books on the shelves.

"You were in the shower, and your mother let me in," Alex said as if he owed an explanation.

He picked up Liam's clothes from the floor and gave them to his friend, who was standing hesitantly in the middle of the room. Alex noticed Liam's uncertainty.

"Dude, I've been swimming and showering with other guys for years. Besides, I've seen what you've got there," he nodded toward Liam's crotch, teasing the embarrassed boy.

Liam didn't budge. He blushed lightly when Alex reminded him of how he'd had to undress in front of Alex after falling into the icy water.

"Okay, okay," Alex said, and he turned around. Liam hated it when Alex embarrassed him by forcing him to strip naked while Alex was watching. Maybe it was something jocks did to dominate the nerdy guys.

Their trip to the mall was a big success. Both boys were able to find the spring clothes they needed, and they tried Vietnamese food for the first time in their lives. They enjoyed their spicy meals. During the ride back to Fairmont, they talked about the action movie they had seen.

"I'm not surprised you are so enthusiastic about Tyler Posey," Alex said after parking on the street in front of Liam's house.

"He played his role well," Liam said, trying to sound casual.

"I am so not buying that. You would watch any movie where he takes his shirt off." Alex was teasing him, but he was right.

They went inside, said quick hellos to Liam's parents, and headed to Liam's room.

"How did you know you were gay?" Alex asked out of the blue. The question surprised Liam, but he decided it was time for the big "gay" discussion. They hadn't really talked about it before.

Liam sat next to Alex on his bed. He opened his mouth to speak but didn't know what to say. The words were stuck in his throat, and he felt his face turning red. The topic was quite personal, and he wasn't used to talking about it. He realized he had actually never talked about it to anybody, not even his parents.

"Well, I just know," he said finally but wasn't satisfied with the answer. Alex waited patiently as if he understood how difficult it was for Liam to talk about this.

"I guess I just find guys good-looking," Liam said. He blushed heavily, and Alex looked at his friend with sympathy.

"Do you find me good-looking?" Alex asked.

Liam's face was red as a fire truck, and he was sweating. "Yes," he answered shyly. "But don't take that the wrong way," he continued, looking worried.

Alex smiled. Liam's confession clearly pleased him. "Don't stress. I already said it's okay with me that you're gay. Besides, there's always room in my fan club," he said, flexing his muscles.

"When did you notice you like guys?" Alex continued.

Liam sighed. "I guess I've always known somehow, but it was a couple of years ago when I fully realized it," he said.

For the first time since moving to Fairmont, Liam talked about Matthew. Alex listened carefully as Liam told him about his childhood friend.

"Have you ever had a boyfriend?" Alex asked after Liam had told him that he and Matthew had never dated.

"No," Liam answered quickly.

He told Alex he would like to have one, but he wasn't ready to date a guy publicly in high school. It wasn't easy for Liam to speak so openly about his most personal feelings, but he was happy to see how comfortably Alex was talking about the topic.

Alex rose and walked to the window. "Do your parents know?" he asked.

"No. You're the only one," Liam replied.

"Isn't it hard to keep it secret?" Alex asked. His eyes were sympathetic.

"Yes, it is," Liam said and felt a teardrop running from the corner of his eye. He was holding in tears.

"I have wanted to tell my parents so many times, but I've never dared to do it," he said after a long pause. "I'm worried they'll kick me out of the house if they find out," he confessed. His eyes were becoming misty.

As he finished his sentence, the door opened and Liam's father looked in. "We are not going to kick you out, but I think we need to talk," he said. Liam looked at his father, frightened.

"Dad," he said, starting to cry. Alex stood there, not knowing what to say.

Chapter 11

Alex drove home and parked his car in front of the garage where his father kept his black Audi. The tall snowdrifts that had dominated the scenery were mostly gone, and only a few small piles of snow were persistently fighting against the sunlight. The garden lighting illuminated the front yard nicely.

He was worried about his friend whose parents had wanted to talk to their son alone. He had gotten to know Mr. and Mrs. Green quite well over the past couple of months, and he hoped Liam wouldn't be in trouble. *Maybe they were just surprised and wanted to talk with him.*

Alex watched how the water that came from the melting snow created bigger and bigger streams when it flowed into the ditch. Suddenly, he remembered how he and Rick had dammed up the water with their tiny plastic shovels. He also recalled his mother's reaction when the boys had run into the house with their muddy rubber boots and rainwear. Alex smiled at the memory. That had been over ten years ago.

He checked his phone, but there were no messages from Liam. He was pondering whether to text his friend when he heard footsteps at the gate.

"Hi, Alex," Sofia said.

Alex stopped tapping his phone and put it into his pocket. "Hi," he said, smiling, and hugged his girlfriend quickly.

"What's up?" he asked merrily, but she just let out an angry snort.

"I want to talk to you," she said.

"I'm here," Alex said, confused. Sofia's expression indicated this answer wasn't good enough.

"Okay, let's go to my room. We can talk there," he proposed finally. His parents were visiting his mother's sister for the weekend, and he was home alone.

Sofia rushed to Alex's bedroom. He picked up a milk carton and a box of cookies from the kitchen and followed her, assuming she would like the chocolate cookies. He and Liam could easily consume a couple of boxes with cold milk while they played video games. Sofia didn't seem interested in them, however, and he put them on the table.

"Do you want to be with me?" she asked bluntly.

There was no need for any empty chitchat with Sofia, and Alex knew where this discussion was going. "I like you a lot," he answered honestly.

She shook her head. "That is just what I mean. You didn't answer my question. I have no clue where we are," she said, her voice growing louder.

"I don't know where we are, either," Alex said and looked down.

"I think I am falling in love with you," Sofia tried again, now calmer and smiling at Alex. "I just feel like you don't want to be with me."

Alex swallowed and sat on the bed next to Sofia. "You are my girlfriend. Of course I care about you," he said.

"But you never have time for me," she hissed and stood up. She seemed to be having trouble containing her anger.

"That's not fair. I have school, swimming practice, and other things in my life," he replied, raising his voice, which he regretted immediately.

Sofia couldn't hold it in anymore. She took the box of cookies and threw it to the floor. The crumbs flew all over the place.

"You have lots of time for Rick," she yelled, "but whenever I want to be with you, your practice is just about to start, or you have homework to do. Not to mention Liam. You just came from his place, didn't you?" Her eyes were full of anger.

Alex was speechless. He felt like there was nothing he could do or say to make it better. There was no denying that Sofia was partially right. They had been on a couple of dates during the past weeks, but their time together was still rather limited. He tried to think of what he could say to keep from losing his girlfriend.

"I asked you whether you still want to be with me, and I want your answer now," Sofia said.

"Yes, I do," Alex answered promptly.

"Good," she said, and a victorious smile rose to her face. Alex sighed. It was looking promising. Apparently, he hadn't lost her.

"Then I want you to stop seeing Liam and spend more time with me," Sofia declared.

"What?" Alex said and jumped up. "You can't be that jealous of my friend," he said, looking at Sofia in disbelief.

She didn't back down. "It's your choice. Me or Liam," she said bluntly and decisively.

"You don't get to tell me who I can be friends with!" he screamed. This time, he didn't regret his angry tone. Sofia was giving him totally unfair conditions for their relationship.

"Fine. We're officially over," Sofia yelled back and marched to the door.

To emphasize her words, she made sure to step on every unbroken cookie on the floor. The love story of the century had ended. Strangely enough, it hadn't ended in tears.

Alex fetched the vacuum cleaner from the utility room and cleaned what was left of the cookies from the floor. He was happy the milk carton was still on the table, untouched. Since he already had the vacuum cleaner there, he ended up cleaning and wiping the dust from his entire room. He was alone in the house, and he had nothing better to do.

Once his room was clean and shining, he dressed in his running clothes and left the house. He ran the path that followed the riverbank. It was already dark, but since the area was rather popular, especially on weekends, the city had installed lights there.

Alex passed some older couples walking on the path, but other than that, he was alone with his thoughts. He was sad that his relationship with Sofia had ended, but it was a relief at the same time. Sofia was without question the prettiest girl in the school, but there were many things about her personality that Alex didn't like. She was shallow and selfish, and she could be mean to people she didn't like.

"Maybe it's better that we broke up…but how am I going to explain this to my teammates?" Alex said to himself. Sofia had asked him to choose between her and Liam, and it would be too easy for his teammates to decide he had chosen the gay guy. He had not really chosen anybody, but he didn't like being given ultimatums.

Actually, the events at Liam's house just before he had left bothered him more than breaking up with Sofia. Liam had been upset, and his father had heard things that he shouldn't have heard. Alex felt that both things were his fault. It was he who started the discussion that had made Liam upset and outed him to his parents. *I wish I had never started that conversation.*

He thought about running to Liam's house but told himself there probably wasn't a third world war going on. Instead, he ran home and checked his phone again for messages from Liam. As there were none, he took a shower.

When he walked from the bathroom to his wardrobe, he saw he had two incoming messages on his phone. The first one was from Rick asking why he and Sofia had broken up. The tone of the message was oddly blaming. He decided to ignore it and talk with Rick at school on Monday.

The second message was from Liam. "Can I come over?" Alex read from the screen.

"Sure," he replied, hoping that everything was okay. Liam's message didn't reveal any details. He went to the kitchen and found the last box of chocolate cookies left. Liam wouldn't throw them to the floor.

"Liam, come here and calm down," his father said after Alex left the house.

Liam wiped his tears and sat in an armchair in their living room. His parents were sitting on a couch opposite him.

"Honey, we're not going to ask you to leave your home," his mother said.

Liam looked at her and then his father. "Thanks, I guess," he said. "So, you're okay with me being…." His words trailed off and it felt impossible to complete the sentence. His parents waited patiently.

"You're okay with me being gay?" he asked quietly and looked down, embarrassed.

"All that matters to us is that you are happy," his mother said. "Actually, we have known it for a long time."

Liam raised his eyes to look at his parents, who were smiling a little. His jaw dropped. "You've known? Why haven't you said anything?"

"Well, of course we didn't know for sure, and we wanted to let you tell us when you felt comfortable," his father answered.

"I wish you had said something. I've want to tell you for so long," Liam sighed.

They hugged each other for a long time and Liam had to wipe his eyes. This time, his tears were happy and relieved, and they felt much better than the sad and painful ones he had experienced just moments ago.

"How did you guess?" Liam asked.

"Your friend Alex is a handsome boy. We've seen how you look at him," his mother said, smiling. Liam's face went red.

"Is he your boyfriend?" his father asked.

"No. We're just friends. Alex has a girlfriend. Sofia," Liam replied.

"What a shame. He would've been such a nice son-in-law," she said.

"Mom!" Liam protested and rolled his eyes.

"Liam, there is still one thing I need to tell you," his father said, getting serious. "We moved here because we thought you might be gay, and we thought it would be easier for you to continue high school here," he said. "I know Fairmont isn't San Francisco, but still."

"You did it for me?" Liam asked, his eyes wide open.

"You are our only son. We love you, and we would do anything for you," his mother said. Liam couldn't hold in his tears anymore. Neither could he count how many times he had cried already.

Liam's mother looked at her son, who seemed reborn. "Are you okay now?" she asked after Liam had wiped his tears again.

"I'm much more than okay," he replied. He hugged his parents one more time before he went to his room and sat on the bed.

It's done. They know, and they still love me! A massive burden dropped from Liam's shoulders, making his whole body shake. Soon, Liam felt like crying again, but he had run out of tears for one day.

"Come have some blueberry pie," Liam's mother shouted from the kitchen. Both Liam and his father arrived quickly. Blueberry pie was their favorite, and they ate and talked for a long time.

I have the best family in the world, Liam thought looking at his parents.

Suddenly he remembered Alex, who had left the house earlier, quite confused. He had to talk to Alex. He texted quickly, and when Alex welcomed him to come over, Liam asked his mother if he could borrow her car. She agreed.

"What did your parents say?" was the first thing Alex asked when he answered the door.

Liam walked inside and repeated most of the conversation to Alex. He left out the parts where they had cried, but Alex couldn't have missed Liam's moist eyes. It amused Alex that Liam's mother had assumed Alex was his boyfriend.

"Do I look that gay?" he said and twisted his wrist.

"That must be the worst gay imitation ever," Liam said and smiled.

"Maybe you need to teach me."

"I am so happy they know," Liam said, growing serious. He was silent for a long time, watching the darkness outside the window.

Alex wrapped his arms around Liam. "I am so happy for you," he said quietly.

Liam was surprised by the hug, and Alex noticed. "You said once that I needed to compensate for all those stupid things I did by hugging you. Consider that my payment," he said, smiling. "Besides, you said it isn't contagious. Don't tell me you were lying."

"You might get an infection if you are exposed to it too much," Liam said and watched as Alex acted scared, withdrawing to the corner of the room. He felt lucky that Alex was so casual about him being gay. Alex was definitely not a dumb jock.

"By the way, I broke up with Sofia today," Alex said, trying to act nonchalant.

Liam could see the breakup was bothering Alex even though he didn't want to admit it. He looked at his friend sympathetically, though he couldn't say he had liked Sofia that much.

"Don't act like it's a big surprise," Alex said. "I'm not really disappointed. I never felt like Sofia was the right one for me. She's pretty and everything, but I'm relieved all that hassle is over."

Unaware that Sofia had asked Alex to choose between Liam and her, Liam pondered if he should say something to comfort his friend. Nothing came out though before Alex changed the subject.

"Wanna play some games?" he asked.

"For sure," Liam replied enthusiastically, and they ran upstairs to Alex's bedroom.

The evening, which had started in a very confusing way, had a happy ending. Liam hoped everything would settle down and stay settled for some time. Little did he know.

Chapter 12

Bright sunlight came in through the big windows when Alex swam the fifty-meter lane from end to end. Finally, he slowed and pushed himself out of the pool. He sat on the edge and drank from his water bottle.

"That was fast!" Eric said. "You'll get a scholarship to some college for sure."

"Coach isn't so optimistic," Alex said, feeling disappointed. "There are plenty of good swimmers this year. A lot more than ever before."

"Then you just need to swim faster," Eric reasoned and patted Alex on his shoulder.

Alex looked out the window at the school's main building on the hill. He wanted to go to a good college, and he was ready to do whatever it took.

He jumped back into the pool and swam as fast as he could. If he needed to beat his old record to get the scholarship, then that is what he would do. Again and again, he sprinted down the lane as Coach Hanson shouted readings from his stopwatch. Finally, the coach ordered the team to finish up and take a shower.

"What's the problem, Alex? That's the slowest I can remember you swimming this year," Coach Hanson said. He had a judgmental tone in his voice Alex didn't like.

"I don't know. I'm trying my best, but I just can't swim faster," Alex said quietly.

"Is everything okay?" the coach asked. His tone had changed completely, and he seemed to be worried.

"Yes, I think so," Alex replied.

"Well, you should take it easy for the rest of the day. Let's try again tomorrow," the coach said. Alex sensed some dissatisfaction in his voice.

"To be honest, you'll need to improve quite a bit to get a scholarship to the best colleges," the coach called, walking toward the locker room. Alex sighed. For a long time, he sat on the edge of the pool with his feet in the water.

When he finally entered the locker room, he saw Rick sitting on the bench. "What the heck are you doing?" Rick asked as Alex stripped off his speedo. Rick had already showered and dressed, and the other boys had left the hall.

"What are you talking about? I'm about to take a shower," Alex answered. He couldn't understand why his taking a shower upset Rick.

"Don't be dumb. Rosa told me you and Sofia broke up," Rick said.

"Yup," Alex said, looking at this friend. He could date whomever he wanted, and it was nobody else's business.

"Do you have somebody else?" Rick asked. "I don't understand. You broke up with the hottest chick in the school," he continued when Alex just shook his head.

"And I don't understand why you are so interested in who I date," Alex said. The discussion irritated him. "Sofia isn't my type. That's all."

"Then who is? Liam?" Rick blurted out.

"What the fuck are you saying?" Alex yelled, glaring at Rick.

"Well, Rosa told me you never had time for Sofia, but I can see you're still hanging out with Liam a lot. Of course, that raises questions," Rick said.

"If having friends makes me gay, maybe I should start avoiding you, too," Alex said.

"Don't twist my words. You know what I mean—or, at least, what I thought when you and Sofia broke up," Rick said. "You know Sofia is Rosa's best friend. Rosa asked me to talk to you," he admitted.

"So, now you are playing a hero in your girlfriend's eyes," Alex said.

Rick could only agree. "Yes, but I was also worried about you. I don't want a fag hanging in the locker room."

"And then you decided to find me a chick so I didn't become gay and spoil your shower experience," Alex snapped and marched to the shower.

"Sorry, Alex. I didn't mean it that way!" Rick shouted from the locker room.

"I think this conversation is over," Alex replied, and he turned on the shower.

Rick's attitude had pissed him off. After taking a quick shower, he dressed and slammed his locker shut with unnecessary force. Then he left the swimming hall. He decided to check if Liam was home, no matter what Rick, Rosa, or Sofia thought about it.

"Hi, come in," Liam said merrily when he opened the door. "How was your practice?"

Alex rolled his eyes and sighed. Liam gave him a questioning look, and Alex decided he had better explain. "I don't think I'll get an athletic scholarship to any decent college," he said sadly.

"How is that a problem?" Liam asked him. "You could easily apply for an academic scholarship. Besides, your parents seem to have plenty of money to pay for your education."

Alex looked at him for a moment. "How are you so smart?" he said as if all his problems were over at once.

Liam smiled. "Some of us are super gorgeous. The rest of us need other skills to survive." He saw Alex blush slightly.

Liam's mother appeared at the kitchen door. "Hi, Alex. Would you like to eat with us? The lasagna will be ready in thirty minutes."

"Thanks. I would be happy to," Alex replied. Swim practice had made him hungry, and he enjoyed having dinner with Liam's family. He liked Liam's parents a lot, and they seemed to like him.

"Nice to have my son-in-law over for dinner," Liam's mother said with a wink.

"Mom!" Liam protested. Now it was his turn to blush. "We are not dating," he shouted to his mother, who had returned to the kitchen. Alex couldn't help laughing.

"Would my boyfriend like to play some video games?" he asked, grabbing Liam's waist and pushing him toward his bedroom. They chose *Call of Duty*, their mutual favorite.

After Liam killed him for the third time straight, Alex looked at his friend. His discussion with Rick in the locker room came into his mind. He couldn't understand why Rick had assumed he was gay—unless Sofia was behind it all and was spreading rumors about him.

He didn't agree with Rick that a gay teammate would be a problem. It was the twenty-first century, and everybody had the right to love whomever they wanted. Besides, Liam was a cool guy and was fast becoming his best friend.

Why do some people behave like we still live in the Middle Ages? he asked himself.

"What are you staring at, so fascinated?" Rosa whispered to Liam, who was sitting next to her in music class.

"Um…nothing," he replied, hoping she hadn't noticed him admiring Eric's muscular body.

"Are you interested in Emily?" she asked, referring to the girl who sat behind Eric. He was happy she hadn't discovered whom he was really looking at, but still, her simple question left him stumbling. At that moment, the class ended.

Liam picked up his stuff and left the room with Rosa. They had become friends, which was a major source of irritation for Rick. Liam enjoyed the situation because Rick had to be on good terms with him to please his girlfriend.

Their next class was geography. The class had moved temporarily to a smaller building on the other side of the schoolyard because their room in the main building was under renovation. They walked across the yard through a heavy wind. Liam smiled instinctively when he saw Eric again in his tight-fitting jeans and Hollister sweater.

"Ouch! That hurt!" Liam said when Rosa jabbed his ribs with her elbow.

"So, it wasn't Emily you were looking at," she said, smiling widely.

Liam felt uncomfortable. She must have seen him checking out Eric. "Um…well, I didn't…or, I-I mean…" he stammered, not really knowing what to say.

"You mean you like boys, and Eric is hot," Rosa blurted with a grin.

"I guess so," he sighed. "I mean…."

"But even though Eric is hot, you are really interested in Alex," she said, continuing to bring facts to the table.

Liam looked at her with his mouth open. "How do you…?" he started.

"How do I know? Well, it's rather obvious. But don't worry, I'm okay with it. It's quite cute, actually. You would be a good couple. It's a shame he's straight," she babbled.

Liam was so confused he almost hit his head on the door of the building where their class was held. He pulled the door open with all his power while the heavy wind tried to keep it shut. They managed to get in.

Did I just come out to her? Liam thought even though, more accurately, Rosa had pulled him out of the closet.

"I really hope he won't continue the boring lecture about air flows and sea powers," she said as they walked to the classroom. Liam was trying to straighten his hair—the wind outside had given him a totally new hairstyle, and he didn't like it.

"You just learned that I am gay, and you are talking about what Mr. Tinkham will teach us today," Liam whispered, pretending to be hurt.

"Don't be such a drama queen! And if you want to surprise me, tell me something I don't already know," she said. They entered the classroom. Mr. Tinkham was already there preparing for class, and he gave them a friendly smile.

"So, you're really okay with this?" Liam asked again, keeping his voice low so nobody else could hear them.

"Yes. I already told you that," Rosa whispered.

"Does Alex know?" she asked. Liam nodded. "Is he, too? I wouldn't have guessed that," she said.

"No, he isn't," Liam said and saw something on her face. Was it disappointment?

Two class periods later, Liam bumped into Alex in the corridor. They were both on their way to history class. Alex smiled at him widely and looked handsome as always.

"Rosa knows I'm gay," Liam whispered when they walked together toward the classroom. Alex stopped and let Liam tell him the whole story.

Alex's face was getting more and more serious. "Are you sure she won't tell Sofia and Rick?" he asked.

Liam could sense something was bothering Alex, but since there was no opportunity for a discussion, he followed Alex to the classroom. They sat together in their familiar places. From the corner of his eye, Liam could see Rosa and Sofia talking with each other at the back of the class. He tried not to think about it; he didn't want to become paranoid.

"Everyone has given their presentations, so it's time to reward the best performance," Mr. Timothy said ceremonially. He took a couple of small trophies out of his bag.

"Holy shit," Liam heard Rick snorting to Eric.

"Mr. Timothy is going to reward the worst ass lickers," Eric whispered back.

Mr. Timothy cleared his throat. "First of all, I want to say that everyone did an amazing job, and I am very proud of you all," he said. He paused dramatically, impressing nobody but himself.

"Liam and Alex, your presentation was the most structured and best prepared. Congratulations!" he said. He held up the trophies and waited for the boys to come and claim them.

Liam was delighted and jumped up immediately. Then he looked at Alex, who rose from his seat slowly, looking very self-conscious and uncomfortable. Avoiding Liam's eyes, he walked to the front of the class where the teacher gave them the trophies and shook their hands formally.

Mr. Timothy started clapping, and the whole class joined in the applause. Rick and Eric clapped their hands slowly once or twice and stared at Liam and Alex. Alex looked at his feet, and he sat silently behind his desk for the rest of the class.

When the class ended, he said to Liam, "I need to go. I have swimming practice. See you tomorrow."

He left quickly before Liam could say anything. There was something strange in his behavior. Was it just the trophies? Or was there something else bothering him?

When Liam walked out of the room, Sofia pushed his shoulder. "Now you've infected my boyfriend. Are you happy?" she said angrily.

"I don't understand," Liam replied.

"Don't play stupid. You can keep him. Have fun!" she said and left. Rosa followed her, looking regretful and embarrassed, barely glancing at him.

"What's wrong with Sofia?" Jacob asked. He had apparently waited for Liam outside the room, though they didn't have chemistry class today.

"Uh…that's a long story. I'll explain later," Liam told him. He wanted to avoid the topic, though he assumed that, by the next day, the whole school would know.

"I can hardly wait," Jacob answered, and they walked together to their lockers.

They separated in the schoolyard, and Liam walked toward his house. He was thinking of Alex. He knew his friend was worried about getting an athletic scholarship, but there must be something else as well. Then Liam realized what it was, and he had to sit down on the bench at a bus stop. How had he missed it earlier?

Alex must be afraid that the whole school would find out Liam was gay. *His teammates won't be pleased when they hear the captain of the swim team is hanging around with a queer.* It would be social suicide for Alex to remain his friend.

The wave of despair that passed through Liam's body was devastating. He realized that it was only a matter of time until he would lose his friend. High school was a cruel game, and Alex had to make his move to keep his position.

Chapter 13

The water felt gooey. With every kick, his feet felt like they were moving in slow motion. His heart was pounding, and he felt exhausted. He inhaled heavily but was still short of breath. Finally, Alex took hold of the lane separator. He had to rest. His performance was unsatisfactory. It would have been pretty obvious to him even if he hadn't noticed how worried the coach looked.

Eric was swimming effortlessly with long pulls. He stopped by Alex and put his hand on Alex's shoulder. "What's wrong? You're swimming like an old grandma or something," he said.

"Everything's okay," Alex said. It wasn't, but he didn't want to talk about it with Eric, or anyone.

"Dude, you need to be at least two or three seconds faster to get a scholarship to Eastwood or any other decent college," Eric said, like Alex didn't know it already.

"I know! I know," Alex said and put on his swimming goggles.

He pushed off from the wall and swam as fast he could. His efforts felt weak, but he had to try. What Liam had told him bothered him a lot. Rosa was a sweet girl, but Alex doubted how long she could keep the knowledge of Liam's sexuality to herself. All hell would break loose if she told Rick.

"One more lap, and then hit the showers," Coach Hanson yelled from the poolside and looked at Alex. "You can stay. I want to talk with you," he added.

The rest of the team finished their lap and left. Alex pushed himself out of the pool and sat on the stand, waiting for the lecture.

"The athletic departments at most colleges will make their decisions very soon. With your current performance, I don't believe you'll get a scholarship," Coach Hanson said.

To Alex's surprise, the coach didn't sound angry at all. Concern was the only thing Alex heard in Coach Hanson's voice. All these years, Alex had assumed the coach couldn't care less about the future of his students as long as he got paid.

"Is there something wrong? Is everything okay at home?" the coach asked hesitantly.

Alex sighed and thought for a long time. Honestly, he didn't know what the problem was with his swimming. The harder he tried, the worse it got.

"Everything is okay," Alex said finally. "Maybe the scholarship thing is just too much pressure."

"You can always talk to me if something is bothering you. You know that, right?" Coach Hanson said and patted Alex on the shoulder.

"Thanks, Coach," Alex replied. He stood and walked to the locker room. There was nothing bothering him—at least, nothing he wanted to talk to the coach about.

He turned on the shower and let the hot water massage his tired shoulders. The water, which normally felt so good, was like a heavy cloak that tried to push him to the floor. He lowered his gaze, crossed his hands behind his neck, and stared at his toes.

He heard somebody talking in the locker room but couldn't make out their words. Soon, Rick and Eric walked into the shower room, wrapped in their towels. Alex could see in their faces that something was wrong, and he had a fair idea of what it was.

"That guy is a fag," Rick hissed.

"Who?" Alex asked nonchalantly, but his muscles tensed.

"Don't play stupid, Wesley. That guy is gay, and you knew it," Rick snorted. He walked toward Alex, and Eric followed him. "Rosa told me everything. There's no need to lie."

"So what?" Alex raised his voice and took a step toward Rick, who was surprised and backed up a couple of steps, almost bumping into Eric.

"Yes. Liam is gay. I've known it for quite a while. So what?" Alex said, looking Rick straight in his eyes.

Nobody said anything for a moment. The boys just watched each other. "So what?" Alex repeated. He was almost shouting now. "Liam is my friend, and I don't give a shit what he is or isn't."

Alex's reaction surprised Rick, who opened his mouth to say something but couldn't find the words. He closed his mouth and looked at Eric for support.

When it became evident that Rick was unable to say anything, Eric asked, "It doesn't bother you to be friends with him, even though you know he's queer?"

"No, it doesn't bother me," Alex said with such confidence that there was no doubt he meant it.

"I think you should focus on getting a scholarship and not on some stupid...Imean..." Rick struggled to express his thoughts. "I mean, hanging out with the f...with the gay guy is making your swimming slower."

"Give me a break," Alex snorted. Rick was about to say something else, but Alex cut him off. "I don't want to hear more stupid shit from your big mouth," he said. Everything about him told Rick and Eric they should leave now.

"Fine," Rick growled, and they left Alex alone in the shower room. "I hope Alex isn't staring at our butts," Rick said, loudly enough for Alex to hear.

"Whatever," Alex muttered and went back to washing his hair.

He spent at least fifteen minutes under the running water, mostly to make sure Rick and Eric had already left the swimming hall before he went into the locker room. He had no interest in seeing cither of them right now, nor could he understand their reaction. Liam had never done anything to harm them.

The first surprise awaited him when he went to the rack to get his towel and swimming trunks. They were nowhere to be found. The second surprise was even less pleasant. The door to the locker room was locked.

"Goddamn Rick," Alex swore. He walked toward the pool area, hoping to find Coach Hanson or somebody with a key. He heard some whistle blows from the hall and was optimistic that the coach of the girls' swimming team could open the door for him.

"Shit," Alex said, realizing he was naked and stopped just as he was about to enter the hall. He walked back to the locker room door and tried to pull it open one more time. No matter how hard he tried, it didn't open. He was trapped naked in the shower room.

Finally, he heard the cleaning lady walking with the floor washer toward the shower room. She was close to his mother's age and dressed in a blue uniform. He had no choice but to walk in her direction and ask for help.

"Do you have a key to the locker room?" Alex asked. The lady looked at the naked boy and smiled widely.

"Have they locked you out?" she asked.

Would I be asking if they hadn't? Alex thought but just nodded.

She pulled the biggest lever on the washer, and it stopped buzzing. Alex followed her to the locker room door, where she took a key chain from her pocket and searched for the right key. "Here you go," she said and returned to her washer. He opened the door and saw his swimming trunks and towel on the floor.

A black Audi was waiting in front of the swimming hall when he finally stepped out of the front doors. "Where have you been?" his mother asked from the passenger seat when he climbed into the back.

"I had a talk with Coach Hanson about scholarships after practice," Alex said, telling the truth selectively.

His father was in the driver's seat. "Your mother and I have decided that we should all go out for dinner since we have a free night," he said. The next thing Alex knew, they were sitting in a restaurant.

"I propose a toast to my son, who will soon be going to Eastwood," Alex's father said after the waitress had brought his red wine.

"We are so proud of you," his mother said, and she raised her glass. They both waited for Alex to lift his glass, which was full of Coke.

"But I haven't gotten any scholarships yet!" Alex said, picking up his drink.

"Such a great athlete will get one for sure," his father said. Alex couldn't remember the last time his father had looked at him with such pride. Maybe never.

"Whatever you say," Alex muttered, so quietly that neither his father nor his mother could hear it.

By the time his cheeseburger arrived, he had lost his appetite. He spent the next thirty minutes surviving his burger. Luckily, his parents were so focused on each other that they paid no attention to him. Over and over again, his thoughts shifted back to the discussion in the locker room.

What does it matter if Liam is gay? What does it matter if anybody is gay? Alex asked himself.

Tick…tick…tick…. Hopeful eyes were following the cheap plastic clock on the wall. The hour hand had moved slowly, but it was finally pointing to five. Alex's swimming practice had finished.

By the time the hour hand reached six, the hopefulness was gone. When the clock showed fifteen past six, it was replaced by endless disappointment. Liam admitted to himself that Alex wouldn't be coming over.

"I can't believe my baby turns seventeen the day after tomorrow! I arranged myself a night off from work. Any requests for your birthday party?" his mother asked cheerfully, unaware of the events of his day.

Liam thought for a moment. Rosa and Jacob would likely accept an invitation from him. Sofia would surely not come. Rick had been rather reserved lately, though most of the time they ate lunch at the same table. Liam would have wanted to invite Matthew, but that wasn't an option.

"I don't think I want a big party. Actually, I'll only invite Alex," he said finally. "And I want a big chocolate cake." His mother smiled and headed for the kitchen.

For weeks, Liam had considered it self-evident that Alex would come to his birthday party. Turning seventeen wasn't a major event for Liam; he had assumed that he would be hanging around with Alex on

Saturday anyway. Hence, he had yet to give Alex the formal invitation.

What if he doesn't want to come? Liam asked himself and felt a sudden, cold rush through his body. He had never had a big gang of friends, but the idea that nobody would want to come and celebrate his birthday was humiliating. He decided to invite Alex first thing in the morning.

When the clock was at half-past six, Liam took out his sheet music and opened the cover of his electric piano. He played "The Clown" by Dmitri Kabalevsky. It was a rather easy song to play—even kids below school age could learn it. But artists at that age were seldom able to bring out the nuances in the piece. They just hit the hammers.

Liam wasn't interested in artistic impression, either. Instead, he tried repeatedly to play the song as fast as he could—and it normally took less than half a minute to play. His fingers hit the keyboard with increasing speed, and his earphones echoed a cacophony that would have made his ears bleed under normal circumstances.

Finally, he was too tired to play anymore, and he went to bed. He considered that, in the morning, the whole school would know he was gay and the rest of his time there would become a total nightmare. Still, the biggest thing that prevented him from sleeping was his uncertainty about why Alex hadn't come over. Something was obviously wrong, and he rolled in his bed for a long time before he finally fell asleep. The hour hand was pointing at two.

Liam was extremely tired when the alarm clock went off at half-past six. He walked like a zombie through the kitchen to the bathroom, and after a surprisingly short shower, he went back to the kitchen to have some breakfast.

"Hello, sunshine. You look cheery this morning," his mother teased.

"Have we run out of cereal again?" he asked, feeling surly.

"Yes, we have. I'll buy more today," she said cheerfully. She knew better than to provoke her petulant son.

"Oh, great. How is that going to help me now?" Liam snorted and slammed the cabinet door. Luckily, he found some ciabatta bread on the table and started to nibble it. He took his bag and left for school.

He arrived well before the first class. He saw Rick and Eric standing under the big maple tree that shaded the front doors, and it was obvious that they had been waiting for him.

"Rosa told us you don't play for our team," Rick said. It took a moment for Liam to realize that Rick was referring to his being gay.

"It's none of your business," he blurted. He had been annoyed already when he left home, and now his annoyance was rapidly growing.

"It is our business. We don't play on your team, and neither does Alex," Eric said.

"We want you to leave Alex alone," Rick said, revealing their ultimatum.

"We don't want anybody on the team hanging out with fags," Eric agreed, pushing Liam heavily on the chest.

Having delivered their message, the boys left before Liam had the opportunity to disagree. Rick stopped at the front door and leaned against it so Liam couldn't go in.

"I hope we understand each other and we don't have to explain this again," Rick said.

"Understood," Liam said quickly. He wanted to go in. Class was about to start, and he didn't want to be late.

"Good. Then we have an agreement," Rick said, looking satisfied.

During the walk to history class, Liam looked at the students who passed by and studied their faces. Nobody paid any attention to him, which meant the entire school hadn't heard the news—at least, not yet.

He had to decide how to react to the ultimatum. It wasn't the first time Rick had bullied him. Fortunately, this time Alex was not part of the problem—unless it was Alex who had asked Rick and Eric to intimidate him, but Liam didn't find that likely.

Since he had already decided not to the let the jocks bully him, he decided to ignore their ultimatum, too. The more important question was whether Alex still wanted to be friends with him.

Mr. Timothy had already opened the classroom door, and most of the students were seated inside. Liam approached his usual seat next to Alex, who saw him and looked worried. Rick and Eric entered the room, watching Liam closely. Liam smiled at Alex and sat next to him, assuming the other boys were not happy.

Liam hardly had a chance to say hello to Alex before Mr. Timothy started the lesson. The teacher emphasized that today's topic was very important for the forthcoming exam, and the whole class began silently taking notes. Ten minutes before the end of the class, Alex raised his hand and asked if he could leave early as he had an appointment with his dentist.

"That's fine," Mr. Timothy said and waited until Alex had left before continuing the lecture. Liam followed Alex with his gaze as he left the class. He stopped staring at Alex's butt only when he realized Rick and Eric were glaring at him.

The class ended soon after, and Liam hurried into the corridor. Strong hands grabbed him from behind, and before he knew it, he had been pushed into the janitor's closet. He heard the door lock, and the lights were switched on.

"So, didn't you understand the agreement we just made?" Rick asked. He kneed Liam's thigh.

"Ouch!" Liam cried and held his leg. The jocks turned on the faucet and pushed his head into the sink.

"Listen, faggot. You—will—leave—Alex—alone!" Rick shouted.

"Okay, I will. Please, stop," Liam begged, sounding miserable as the water flowed over his hair and shirt.

The jocks looked at each other and decided that Liam had understood the message. Reluctantly, they let go of him and left the closet. Liam found some hand towels and tried to dry his hair and face. Once ready, he limped out of the closet.

"Has something happened?" Mr. Timothy asked. He saw the awkward way that Liam was walking.

"Nothing serious. I just ran into a table when I left class," Liam lied, grateful that Mr. Timothy hadn't paid attention to his wet hair. He walked toward the lockers before the teacher could engage him in further discussion.

After he had closed his locker, he looked around. He couldn't see Rick or Eric anywhere. Assuming Alex was still at the dentist, he took his cell phone from his pocket. He sent a text to Alex that read, "My mother is planning a birthday party for me tomorrow at 3 pm. Welcome!"

Half an hour later, he received a reply. "OK, thx." He hoped it meant that Alex was coming.

Chapter 14

The drill made Alex's skull tremble. The dentist had been working on the tooth for fifteen minutes, despite repeated promises that it would soon be over. Alex didn't mind. He wasn't particularly scared of the dentist, and he had a rather high threshold for pain. Besides, most of his face was numb from the anesthetic.

"We're done now. That's all," the dentist said after another fifteen minutes. She was an elderly lady, close to retirement.

Alex thanked her politely for the treatment and left for school. Suddenly he remembered that his phone had vibrated in his pocket just before the dentist had started to push the massive needle into his gum. He read the message about Liam's birthday and replied quickly. Then he had to run since he was already late for chemistry class.

When he arrived, the teacher opened the classroom door for him, and Alex took his seat next to Rick. They had been sitting together for the entire year, even during their recent friction. Rick had already organized all the equipment on the table and was setting fire to the gas burner. Carefully, he added one spoonful of sodium sulfate to the liquid in the petri dish and mixed it with a glass stick.

"Eric and I made sure the fag won't bother you anymore," Rick whispered as he took the pipette to fill the test tube.

"What?" Alex shouted, regretting the outburst immediately when half of the class turned to look at him. He waited until everyone went back to their chemistry work and asked again, whispering this time, "What did you do?"

"Don't worry. We took care of your problem."

Alex didn't like the smirk on Rick's face, and as soon as the class was over, he pushed Rick and Eric out of the classroom to a place where other students couldn't listen.

"What the fuck did you do?" Alex asked and glared at his friends.

"Alex, we're a team," Rick said. "You are our star swimmer, and we want to win Eastern Regionals."

"And what does that have to do with Liam?" Alex asked.

"That has everything to do with Liam!" Rick said quickly, staring at Alex. "With all due respect, Mr. Captain of the Team, your swimming has really sucked since you started hanging out with that queer," he added with zero respect in his voice.

"Besides, any friends of that fag are not welcome in the locker room," Rick continued, and Eric nodded.

"You can't be serious," Alex said and looked at both boys. The looks on their faces told him that they were.

"The choice is yours. It's either us or the fag. If you keep hanging out with that queer, you're not welcome on the team," Eric said.

Alex was furious. It was the second time he had heard that ultimatum: first from Sofia, and now from Rick and Eric.

"It's none of your business who I'm friends with," Alex said and pushed Eric against the wall. "If Liam is a threat to your manliness, then you're much smaller people than I ever imagined. Grow up!" he said and marched off.

Alex walked to his locker and kicked the door so hard that everybody in the hall turned to look at him. He didn't care. Sofia had been his girlfriend, and Rick and Eric were some of his oldest friends. Now he was losing them all. And all of this was because of Liam, who had just moved to Fairmont.

The swim team was his second family, but there was something in Liam, which made it hard for Alex to end their friendship. He knew exactly what it was, but he didn't want to say it aloud.

Alex walked out to the parking lot and opened the door of his car. He would skip the rest of his classes. The time had come to make a decision.

It was Liam's seventeenth birthday tomorrow. Alex knew exactly what gift he would buy to Liam, so he drove to the mall. He found it easily at a decoration store, but holding it in his hands made him feel nervous. *It is now or never*, he thought.

The salesclerk wrapped the gift in nice paper. "She's a lucky girl," the clerk said and smiled at Alex. "Um… yes, she is," Alex replied and blushed.

Alex returned to his car but didn't start the engine. What the salesclerk had said troubled him.

He had known it for some time and had done his best to ignore his feelings, but he couldn't do that anymore. His hands were shaking, and he took hold of his wrist with his other hand. *I'm gay and that's why I never really wanted to date Sofia.*

Sofia had chased Alex for a long time before Alex finally agreed to date her. For him, it had felt more like an obligation than something he really enjoyed. He had felt like the entire world expected him to date her. So he had, and it had been a mistake. Luckily, it was over now.

Liam was the kindest person Alex knew. They had spent a lot of time together lately, and Alex appreciated their friendship. Still, Alex wasn't sure what he should do. Maybe it was best to hide his feelings from everybody. Maybe he and Liam were not meant to be more than friends.

Liam didn't think turning 17 was all that big of a deal. Lazily, he crawled out of bed and pulled the curtains.

Even the brightness of the Saturday morning didn't cheer him up. Alex's behavior was bothering him.

Since learning that Rosa knew Liam was gay, Alex had hardly spoken to him. Also, it troubled him that it might have been Alex who had sent Rick and Eric to intimidate him. What other reason could Rick and Eric have had to say those things? Why didn't Alex break off his friendship with Liam himself? Why had he left school in the middle of the day yesterday?

Liam's head was full of questions and he had no answers. He had last seen Alex in history class but had heard nothing from him since. He still hoped that Alex might come to his birthday party, but the hope was so fragile that he didn't want to break it by calling Alex and asking.

"Oh, there's my pumpkin. Happy birthday!" his mother fussed and hugged Liam when he arrived in the kitchen for breakfast.

"Happy birthday," his father said, pouring himself more coffee.

"Thanks," Liam muttered and opened the cupboard. Luckily, there was some cereal this time.

After Liam had eaten, his mother passed him an envelope. "Your father and I have a small gift for you," she said. Liam looked at the envelope, unsure of whether he was expected to open it.

"We thought you might need some new clothes and you might want to choose them yourself," his father said. Liam's eyes opened wide when he saw how much money his parents had put in the envelope.

"Thanks!" he said, jumping up to hug his mother. "You're the best."

"Even though it's your birthday, I need you to help me clean the house for the party," his mother said.

"That's okay," Liam replied. He didn't have anything else to do but to worry about whether Alex would come. Any distraction was more than welcome.

"We have quesadillas for lunch," his mother said. "And your cake is already in the fridge. I hope Alex likes chocolate cake." Tortillas were Liam's favorite, and his spirits had been high until the mention of Alex sent it into a major tailspin.

"Um…I'm not sure whether Alex will come," he said tentatively, and his mother looked at him, amazed.

"Is he busy today?" she asked. Liam hesitated for too long, and she pressed him. "Have you had a quarrel or something?"

"No, nothing like that," Liam said. He could give no reasonable explanation as to why Alex might not come. "He has just been a little odd lately. I hope he comes," he said finally.

"He better come. He'll have to deal with me if he misses my son's birthday party," she said with such determination that Liam had to smile a little.

They cleaned the house and Liam started with his bedroom. First, he gathered all his comic books and stacked them on a shelf. A moment later, he put them back on the floor and started to organize them in chronological order. When he was happy with the outcome, he arranged them in piles on the shelf.

Liam was about to delete the unnecessary files from his laptop but decided that his mother's definition of cleaning couldn't possibly be extended to that task. Instead, he arranged his laptop nicely on the table before getting the vacuum cleaner to remove the dust from the floor.

A couple of hours later, the house started to look neat and orderly. "You guys have done an amazing job," Liam's mother said to Liam and his father. "Lunch will be served in ten minutes," she announced.

Liam was sweaty and needed a shower. Cleaning the house had been much harder work than he had anticipated. However, it had offered him a comforting break from worrying about Alex.

After drying himself with a big white towel, he took his best clothes from the wardrobe. He wanted to look nice when Alex came. Thinking about Alex made him smile again, and he decided to stop worrying so much. Alex was his friend. Surely, he would come to his party.

"These tortillas are ridiculously good," Liam said as his family sat at the table, enjoying their lunch. His mother looked satisfied.

"I am happy to hear that," she said. She reached over to ruffle his hair before remembering how important perfect hair styling was to Liam. She pulled back her hand.

"Great. You're learning," Liam said when he realized his hair had survived the impending attack. His father laughed.

After his third tortilla, Liam thanked his mother again for the great lunch and set his plate in the sink.

He looked at the clock on the wall. It was half-past two, which meant Alex would arrive soon. Liam spent the next half hour in his bedroom, walking around nervously and looking out the window.

Soon it was three, but there was no sign of Alex. At five minutes past three, Liam assumed Alex was on his way and would arrive soon. At fifteen minutes past three, he became somewhat worried. By half-past three, the endless disappointment could be read on his face. Alex wasn't coming.

Liam's mother appeared at the door and saw his sad face. "I'm sorry. Maybe Alex has a good reason for being late," she said, giving him a weak smile.

"No, he doesn't. He doesn't want to be friends with me anymore," Liam said. It was time to accept reality. His mother asked what had happened between the boys, but Liam said he didn't want to talk about it right now.

"Would you still like some cake?" she asked.

Liam didn't answer but walked bravely to the kitchen after his mother. He had lost his appetite, and as great as the cake must have been, he didn't taste anything. All his senses were numb. He ate the cake bite by bite, holding back his tears.

When he had finally eaten the tiny piece he had cut from the enormous cake, he tried to smile at his mother. Then he shuffled back to his bedroom, closed the door, and drew the curtains.

An old t-shirt hanging on the back of his chair reminded him of Matthew. Until their separation, Matthew had spent every birthday with him. The shirt was the last present his friend had given him before disappearing from his life. He wished that Matthew was with him now, celebrating his birthday.

Liam thought he might watch a movie, so he turned on the TV and randomly picked a DVD from the shelf. The movie started to play, but he felt like he was watching it from behind a thick layer of fog. His eyes filled with tears, and Liam folded his arms around his legs. The scene on the TV became meaningless, and he just sat on his bed and cried inconsolably.

Chapter 15

After sitting half an hour in his car, Alex finally started the engine and left the mall. His math class had begun already, but after the chat with Rick and Eric, he knew that he just couldn't be there. Instead, he drove back home. He wasn't thinking clearly and didn't realize that coming home was a mistake until he got there. As soon as he opened the front door, he saw his father in the hall. They looked at each other.

"Why aren't you at school?" his father asked.

Shit. Alex was too startled at finding his father at home to come up with an excuse. He just stared, speechless. "I'm not feeling well," he said finally.

It was partially true but not exactly the reason he had skipped his classes. His father scanned Alex for hints of whether he was telling the truth. Finally, he just nodded.

"Let's make some chicken soup," his father said. "I'm hungry, and it might make you feel better." Alex followed him to the kitchen. They collected all the ingredients, and Alex started to fry the chicken in a pan.

"How is it going with Sofia? I haven't seen her here for a while," his father asked casually while pouring coconut milk into the boiling water.

"We broke up," Alex said.

"Oh…well, teen romances seldom last forever." His father sounded like he was talking from experience. "Is that why you don't feel well?" he asked.

"No, that's an old story," Alex replied and lowered the heat to make sure the chicken didn't burn.

They got the soup ready, and Alex set the table. He didn't want to talk about his separation with Sofia or his disagreements with Rick and Eric, so they ate in silence. Unfortunately, as soon as his father had spooned the last bit of his soup into his mouth, he decided to continue talking.

"Have you heard anything about the scholarship?" he asked.

Alex didn't feel comfortable telling his father that he was unlikely to get one. "No, not yet," he said.

"Okay. I'm sure they will inform you soon."

The more they talked, the more Alex felt there were things in his life that he didn't want to share with his parents. It was a heavy feeling. Sooner or later, his father would find out about the scholarship. After the events of that morning, he wasn't even sure he wanted to continue on the swim team, which would be another major disappointment for his father.

Probably not the biggest, Alex thought and looked at the old man, who was now collecting the dishes from the table.

Alex walked to his room, feeling much worse than he had before eating the magic healing soup. He picked up his history book and tried to do some homework but found it impossible to concentrate. Soon, he gave up and put the book back into his bag. He turned on the TV and watched some stupid early-afternoon soap operas.

At three-thirty, he texted his coach, saying he was sick and wouldn't be participating in swim training today. Coach Hanson didn't reply, which wasn't unusual for him. Alex was sure Rick and Eric would interpret his absence as a clear sign that he had made his choice.

His mother came home at half-past six, and they ate dinner. The meal was something she had grabbed on her way home. It was okay, but Alex's mind was somewhere else. Somehow, he managed to get through dinner without too much drama.

Afterward, Alex tried again to do some homework, this time with slightly more success. He couldn't help thinking about how grateful he was to Liam for helping him with school. Maybe he could still get an academic scholarship if he didn't get an athletic one.

Alex woke up just before ten the following morning. His parents had eaten breakfast a couple of hours earlier and left to go shopping at the Buonas mall. Alex didn't expect them to come home until the evening since his mother had left him some lasagna in the fridge for lunch.

It was a silent morning, and Alex decided to make the most out of it. After going for a jog, he played some video games and started to watch the third *Lord of the Rings* movie on DVD. It was one of his favorites, and he lay casually on the sofa with a big glass of Coke and a bowl of microwave popcorn.

Suddenly, he jumped up and looked at the clock on his cell phone. It was almost four. He was late for Liam's birthday party. Within a minute, he had turned off the television, changed into better clothes, and jumped into his car.

"How could I be so stupid?" he asked himself. Luckily, it was a rather short drive to Liam's house.

Liam's mother answered the door, not looking particularly happy, but she smiled quickly and let Alex in. The door to Liam's bedroom was closed, and Alex opened it carefully and stepped in. Liam glanced at him. His eyes were red, and his face was wet from tears.

"I thought you didn't want to come," Liam said in a voice barely louder than a whisper.

"I'm really sorry. I was watching a movie and didn't realize the time. It's all my fault," Alex said.

Alex sat on the bed next to Liam and hugged the tearful boy. Gently, he put Liam's head against his chest and let him cry.

"You're my best friend. Of course I want to come to your birthday party," Alex said when Liam's sobbing started to fade away. Liam stopped crying but remained against Alex and rested his head on his shoulder.

They sat in silence and watched the movie that was playing on the TV. Alex wondered frantically whether he should say something but decided to let Liam fully calm down first. He had apparently been very upset.

Fifteen minutes later, Alex became aware of Liam taking his head away from his shoulder and leaning away from him.

"Sorry. I didn't mean to come on to you," Liam said, embarrassed.

Alex didn't mind the intimate position and pulled him back wrapping his arm around him. "Come here. It's your birthday," he said.

"Well, if I have your permission," Liam said and lowered his head back to Alex's shoulder. They kept watching the movie in total silence. Neither of them felt the need to speak. Everything was okay again.

The hand that Alex had wrapped around Liam was on Liam's thigh. Liam turned and glanced at Alex, embarrassed. Even though it was dark, Alex could see that he was blushing.

"Please don't be scared, but I have to adjust it a little bit," Liam said.

"Adjust what?" Alex teased him.

"Well…you know," Liam replied, and his face got even redder. He adjusted his crotch quickly.

"I guess I have to do it, too," Alex said casually and put his hand inside his jeans. Liam glanced at the bulge in Alex's jeans and raised his eyes to Alex's face. He looked so confused that Alex almost laughed.

"I guess it likes you," Alex said shyly. "Actually, I am sure it likes you, and I like you, too. I mean, I like you in that way," he added, pointing to his jeans. Liam started to smile, and it was the widest smile that Alex had ever seen on that face.

A half-naked Taylor Lautner was running on TV, but Liam didn't see it. He was far too focused on Alex, his beautiful eyes and hair, not to mention his hot body. He didn't know what to do or what to say. He wasn't even sure what he had just heard Alex say or what it meant.

"You mean that…?" Liam started to ask. A large part of him was hopeful. The other part was afraid he had misunderstood and that his world would collapse at any second. It didn't. Alex nodded.

"I've been thinking about it a lot over the last couple of weeks or so. And I think that I play on the same team as you," Alex said. "At least, it feels good to be with you. It never felt like this with Sofia," he added. He tightened the hold of his arm that was wrapped around Liam.

"Wow," Liam said quietly. He repeated it a couple of times and looked at Alex again, still unsure of what to do or say. Alex was watching him and obviously had something in mind. Liam raised his eyebrows and gave him a questioning look, hoping to encourage him.

"Would you like to be with me? I mean, would you like to be my boyfriend?" Alex asked quietly. He blushed. "I mean, I understand if you don't want to," he added quickly. He was about to continue when Liam raised his hand to stop him from speaking.

"Yes," Liam said and gazed into Alex's eyes. "I have wanted to be your boyfriend since the moment we met," he said, keeping their eye contact.

Alex moved his head closer to Liam and hesitated for a moment. Then they kissed. It might have been, technically, a clumsy kiss, but Liam felt it in his whole body. "Wow."

For a long time, the boys sat side by side on Liam's bed, Liam resting his head on Alex's shoulder. He felt happier than ever before in his young life. The handsome jock had just kissed him and wanted to be his boyfriend. If this was a dream, he never wanted to wake up.

"Um…just one more thing," Alex said and looked uneasy. "Is it okay if we keep this just between us?"

"That's okay," Liam said, and he felt how Alex's body relaxed. "I guess Rick and Eric will make sure the whole school knows about me soon. But they don't have to know about us."

Alex sighed. "It's not fair to put only you in the spotlight. I feel like a coward," he admitted and looked away. Liam hugged him and stroked his hair. He was surprised at how vulnerable the big jock felt in his hands.

"I don't mind. Let's not worry about it now," Liam said. "As long as I have you, I can cope with whatever crap they give me," he added confidently.

They kissed again. "Happy birthday to my super cute…boyfriend," Alex whispered in Liam's ear.

Epilogue

Alex woke up in his bed on Sunday morning. He smiled. He had a boyfriend, which felt exciting and scary. And, most importantly, it felt right. He had never felt the same about Sofia, and now he understood why. *I'm gay*, Alex thought, and the finality of the statement made gooseflesh prickle his skin.

He couldn't stop thinking about Liam. His face was so cute when he was thinking hard about something, and his smile was something Alex could have gazed at for hours and hours. Liam was also small and skinny, which made him beautiful in Alex's eyes.

Alex knew he had a lot of unfinished business with Rick and Eric. Going to school on Monday morning wouldn't be easy, especially for Liam, but Alex had promised to protect him. The boys would no longer welcome him on the swim team.

He knew he had to talk about the scholarship with his parents. He had put off the topic for too long because he felt he would disappoint his father, who had high hopes for his athletic career.

But all that would be another story. Today, Alex just wanted to be happy and in love with Liam. Nothing could feel better than that.

About the Author

Jay Argent is a novelist in his forties who lives a peaceful life with his husband. His favorite hobbies are music, movies, and romantic novels. He obtained a degree in engineering in 2001 and built a successful career in a management consulting firm. Using his own high school and college experiences as inspiration, he is now pursuing his true passion of writing.

If you have any feedback, you can contact him by email at jay@jayargent.com. He very much looks forward to hearing from you.

www.jayargent.com

Printed in Great Britain
by Amazon